DEAD NIGHT

FOUR FITS OF FEAR

KRISTI HELVIG   SUE DUFF   A.G. HENLEY
CORINNE O'FLYNN

Wicked Ink Books
Colorado USA
www.wickedinkbooks.com

DEADNIGHT
FOUR FITS OF FEAR

CORINNE O'FLYNN

KRISTI HELVIG

A.G. HENLEY

SUE DUFF

For our readers
Something creepy this way comes . . .

CONTENTS

THE MISSING

KRISTI HELVIG

THE MISSING

JESS CHEWED OFF A PIECE OF CHERRY LICORICE AND frowned. "Doesn't look so scary to me."

"I bet it's way creepier in the dark." Sam cocked her head to the side and stared.

The intricate hexes that dotted the doorways of the houses looked more faded and sad than ominous. The round paintings, about the size of a dinner plate each, were centered above each door and consisted of stars, flowers, and animals as far as Jess could tell. She didn't see what the big deal was.

The houses looked identical to the ones in her subdivision down the road—traditional two story homes, most with small but cute porches and some stone and brick on the front sides to make it look all fancy

Jess shrugged. "It's like any other cookie-cutter neighborhood in suburbia—just with eccentric home décor preferences." She gestured toward one house from where they stood in the middle of the street. "I mean, look at the designs, Sam. These people probably do those lame adult coloring books."

Sam giggled then stopped as she stared into the trees. "Yeah, but you heard what Colton said . . . about the demon."

"He just wants to scare you so he can save you . . . by getting into your pants at Mike's party." Jess flashed her a wicked grin as she bit off another piece of licorice. The big end-of-senior year party was happening at Mike's house Friday night while his parents were off on some last-ditch divorce prevention retreat in California.

Sam smacked Jess's arm. "Does not." She looked at the houses again and her face grew somber. "But seriously, that girl, Emily, who went missing here . . . and the other girl before her. Not to mention all those kids in the next county . . ." She trailed off as she stared at the thick woods that crept up to the edge of neighborhood.

Jess shook her long blond hair. "Oh please, it was the 80's . . . everyone went missing back then. It's not like they had these to track you." She waved her smartphone around in its hot pink case with a glitter peace sign.

Sam continued to stare off into the trees beyond the last house on the cul-de-sac—the one where Emily had lived. They walked closer. The paint on the house was a dull grey color. The yard was mowed but it looked like the upkeep was kept to a bare minimum.

The rest of Emily's family, her parents and younger brother, had stayed there after her disappearance, supposedly in the hopes that Emily would return. The brother grew up, went off to college, got married, and moved to the East Coast, but his parents had stayed, refusing to give up hope. They still lived there—or so the rumor said. No one knew much about the other girl who had gone missing a few years before that. Just that her family moved away right after and never came back.

Jess noted the bright paint of the hex against the grey. It was the one hex that had been carefully maintained. Maybe the other neighbors had painted theirs as a sign of support at the time, like how those kids on the news shaved their head to support the guy with cancer in their class. Then after some time had passed, and no other girls went missing, the hysteria and superstitions about the demon died down and the neighbors let the hexes fade along with their fears.

Jess swallowed her licorice and took a step closer to Sam who stood at the driveway of the grey house. She spoke in a low voice. "But maybe you're right, Sam . . . no girls have disappeared since Emily, so the hexes must have worked." Her friend seemed transfixed by the dark woods.

Jess had to admit that the forest seemed to swallow the light of the bright day. She shook her head—what was she thinking? Trees were trees. She whispered in Sam's ear. "That demon who preys on girls in the night must be really, really hungry after all these years. Like . . . famished." She gripped Sam's arm and Sam shrieked.

Jess jumped back. "Shhh . . . could you be any louder? Someone's gonna call the cops."

Sam shook off Jess's hand. "That wasn't funny at all." She looked around. "Let's get out of here. I don't like this place." She turned and stormed back toward her car that she had parked between two houses about a block away.

"Suit yourself." Jess jogged to catch up with her. "Geez, it was just a joke. That whole story is an urban legend. You know, like, the guy with the hook for an arm who killed couples while they were making out in their cars."

Sam's face was set in a grim line. She didn't respond as she pressed the button on her key fob to unlock the car and slid into the driver's seat.

Even after Jess got in, Sam wouldn't talk and only turned up the radio as they drove out of the neighborhood. Jess would have admitted the creepiness of the story—the fact that their neighborhood sat only a mile away from this one was kind of weird—but did Sam have to be so uptight? Jess held up her phone and snapped pics of several houses.

Sam sighed. "What are you doing?"

"This is so going on my Instagram. Can't let these hexes go to waste." Jess smiled sideways at her friend. "Plus, I got you to talk to me."

Sam shook her head as she drove. Jess stifled a laugh because as mad as Sam was, she didn't go a mile over the speed limit. Jess put down her window and let the wind mess up her hair. They turned onto Jess's street—only two streets away from Sam which had made it easy to walk to each other's houses before Sam got her license and they decided walking wasn't cool. Jess had the embarrassing problem of having a license but no vehicle. Technically, her dad had a car but since he worked two jobs, it wasn't available much.

"Are we good?" Jess asked.

"No, I'm still mad at you." Sam turned into the driveway.

"Fine, but we're going to Mike's party together tomorrow night. Right?"

Sam responded with a shrug.

Jess got out of the car. "We are going . . . it's THE LAST party of the year—our senior year! You can't stay mad forever." She held her hand on the door. "But really, I'm sorry if I scared you."

Sam didn't respond, so Jess reluctantly shut the door. As her friend pulled away from the curb, Jess turned and yelled toward the open window "It's 2018, Sam—demons aren't real!"

JESS SURVEYED herself in her bathroom and nodded with approval. The straightening iron had worked magic on her hair which hung in a smooth golden sheet over her shoulders. *Pouty Pink Perfection* glossed her lips and the black kohl eyeliner made a smoky rim around her blue eyes. Her jeans had taken fifteen minutes to wriggle into; she was pretty sure that breathing would be a challenge the rest of the evening.

This was the night—the night Jake would finally kiss her. He had totally checked her out today in World Lit. She still felt the burn of his gaze on her legs, which she'd shown plenty of in her short denim cutoffs. She'd totally broken dress code policy but had made it under the radar. It would have been worth the detention. She'd been trying to get Jake's attention all year, and today was her lucky day.

Her mother would have said that it was more important for a boy to pay attention to her mind than to her legs. That a boy who only noticed your legs wasn't worthy of your attention. But her mother had died of cancer when she was thirteen. Her voice had grown fainter and fainter in Jess's head, until she wasn't sure she heard it at all anymore.

She grabbed her phone and punched at the screen.

U still picking me up at 8? Girl, hope ur ready to party

Sam hadn't been in school today but Jess wasn't worried. She'd never been able to stay mad at Jess for long and wouldn't skip school. In fact, Sam loved

school. The only reason she'd miss school was if
—oh crap.

The next text confirmed Jess's worst fear.

Sorry, I'm not going. I've been super sick all day.

Sam. Even when sick, she wrote grammatically
correct texts. She was sorry Sam was sick, but really?
Sam knew how important tonight was for Jess. This
was not happening. She tried again.

C'mon, itz the last party of the year
It will help u feel better

For good measure, she inserted emojis of
balloons, hearts, and a party blower at the end.

I'm puking, Jess. My fever is so high that I'm literally
sweating out my Diet Coke. I know you want to see Jake,
so I'm sure you can find another ride.

Jess wondered if Sam was trying to make her feel
selfish. It's not like she only wanted Sam for a ride—
they'd been best friends since kindergarten. They
did everything together. This party had been all
they'd talked about for the past few weeks. Okay,

maybe Jess had done most of the talking but Sam had seemed excited too. She didn't want Sam to be sick or mad at her.

Feel better I'll text u 2morrow

When all Sam texted back was "*K*," she knew her friend must be really sick not to type out the whole word. Jess sighed. It was almost eight; the party would be getting into gear soon. She texted Rachel and Emma from homeroom, since they were all meeting up at Mike's.

Samz sick. Can I catch a ride with u?

Her heart sank with the reply.

We're already here. Get over here—this place is hopping.

They were friends but not the type of friends she could ask to leave and come get her. Sam was the only friend she had like that. She couldn't ask her dad because he was working the night shift at the store again. He'd taken all the extra shifts he could get after Mom died. Jess didn't know if it was due to needing the money, or if it was an escape. Either way, he was never around. Which meant the car wasn't either.

She texted a few other classmates but either got no response or they were already at Mike's. Great. Everyone was there except her. She checked her phone. Pics were already going up on Insta. Was that Jake in the background? No way was she missing out on this party. She had put too much effort into her hair to let a lack of a ride stop her.

Jess pulled up the map app on her phone and typed in the address. It hurt to see that it would only take fifteen minutes to get there by car. The bus graphic was useless as there were no busses in this part of suburbia. She took a breath—as much as she could in the stomach crushing jeans—and clicked the walk icon. One hour and fifteen minutes away by walking. Nope.

There was only one thing left to do and her mother was not here to talk her out of it. She took one last glimpse of herself in the mirror, flashed a victory sign, and walked outside. With the sun down, there was a slight chill in the hair. Jess thought about taking her jacket, but it ruined the look of the sequined tank top she'd perfectly paired with her jeans. Plus, she didn't want to carry it around all night. She looked down at her strappy wedge sandals. They were definitely not ideal for walking, but she didn't plan to walk far, and these sandals were too cute to leave behind. She could almost look the six foot tall Jake in the eyes.

Jess shoved the phone into her back pocket and walked down the street of her subdivision. It wouldn't really be hitch-hiking because they were technically her neighbors—just ones she might not know. It's not like she was asking total random strangers for a ride. She'd seen that done in a movie once, where they stuck out their thumb to get a ride, but it was so 80's. She would just wave at cars until one stopped. Easy peasy.

She'd gone about four blocks when she was forced to reach down and adjust her sandal strap. It dug into her ankle and although it was dark, she could feel the raw welt under the strap. Maybe she should go back for a Band-Aid. *Or more sensible shoes.* Her mother's voice. It had been months since she'd heard that comforting voice in her head. A tear threatened to drop from Jess's deeply mascaraed eyelash. "Nope." Jess flicked the tear away. "Too much work went into this face."

She would just have to suck it all up—the walking, the shoes like sandpaper against her ankle, the not-being-where-Jake-was yet. Where were all the cars? Some Friday night. Maybe everyone was either lame and staying home—it was suburbia after all—or they were out already.

Jess reached the exit of her subdivision and turned on to the county road. It was freaky to go from all the street lights and houses of the subdivision to . . . basically nothing. No lights, no houses. Almost total darkness. Jess let her eyes adjust to the dark and looked upward. She could just make out a few stars, and the moon was a sliver in the sky. Sam would be so scared. She'd totally be talking about demons by now.

She kept walking while wishing a car would come by. The searing pain on top of her ankle demanded her attention, and when Jess leaned down to loosen the strap, it was wet. Perfect. She was bleeding. Bloody sandals were the opposite of super cute. Jess stopped and removed both shoes. She looped the straps over her fingers and carried them. She'd have to put them back on when she got to the party. Her sparkly tank was so fabulous that no one would notice her feet anyway.

Jess shivered in a cool breeze. *Why didn't you bring your jacket?* There was mom again. She thought back to her mother pushing her on the swing as a child; reading her fairytales at night; brushing her hair before bed. All too soon it became Jess's turn to brush her mother's hair when she didn't feel well—at least until it all fell out from the chemo. As her mom grew thinner and weaker, and no longer had the focus or energy to read, Jess sat on the side of her bed and read books to her. In the end, she could only hold her mother's hand each day while she waited for the morphine to ease her pain. Cancer sucked.

A car whizzed by while Jess was lost in thought. She turned toward the red taillights driving away from her. "Dangit to bits!" she yelled. "I need a ride!"

Jess pulled the phone from her back pocket to check the time. 8:30. Jake would have had a beer or two by now, and surely, there were other girls there in tight jeans and tank tops who might have caught his attention. Maybe they'd already gotten him another drink and stood by him right now, flipping their hair and laughing at whatever he said. Leaning into him and touching his arm as they flirted.

"Not on my watch," Jess announced, as she opened her map app again. The red dot where Mike's house sat still seemed so far away. The county road wound around the town, looping to several subdivisions along the way. Jess studied the brightly lit screen. At least she still had good service out here.

She had two hours to go if she walked this way, and her odds hadn't been good so far. Jess could either keep going and chance finding a car—or find a short cut. She enlarged the map. If she went another half mile, she would reach a neighborhood on her right where she could cut through the woods. Mike's house looked to be a straight shot once she hit the other side.

Jess froze. That neighborhood was *the* neighborhood. The straight shot would involve walking right past Emily's house on the cul-de-sac . . . into the same woods where Sam was convinced a demon lived. Jess didn't scare easily, but she'd also never told Sam about the missing person photo of Emily she'd found online. It must have been a school photo because Emily had that same blue backdrop that she'd had in her own photo. What creeped Jess out was Emily's likeness to Jess—from the wavy blond hair to the blue eyes. They could have been sisters.

About a year ago, she'd heard about a group of seniors at her school who went to sleep in those woods on a dare. They hadn't gone far into the forest and made it about an hour before one of the girls had a meltdown and ran out of the trees screaming that something was wrong. The boys and two other girls who'd been there had run out of the forest right behind her. None of them would talk about what happened.

It would have been better if the moon were full —at least there would have been some light to guide her. She had the flashlight app on her phone but didn't want to drain the battery in case she really needed it. A fleeting thought entered her mind to turn around and go back home. *Yes, go home, Jess. Please.*

Jess ran her fingers through her hair. She was tired, her ankle was bleeding, and now she wasn't just chilled—she was cold. The temperature must have dropped several more degrees and the breeze had grown into a steady wind. She could curl up on the couch under a blanket, eat caramel rice cakes, and binge watch Netflix.

Jess hesitated. She stopped mid-step and looked back over her shoulder, unsure what to do. Then fate intervened.

Yo, it's Jake. Emma gave me ur number. R u coming?

Excitement flooded her body, giving Jess renewed energy and determination. Her fingers were cold as she texted back.

On the way. Don't suppose u can give me a ride?

She down stared at her phone as she walked. Please say yes. Please say yes.

Nah, sorry. Got a lift with Chris and don't know where he's at.

It was fine. Jess was almost at the entrance to Emily's neighborhood. She turned right into the subdivision. It wouldn't be long now.

No worries. Almost there—be there in 30

Jake texted back immediately.

Cool. C ya soon.

She smiled. His texts were surely a sign—it was going to be the best night ever.

JESS'S quick steps slowed as she neared the end of the last street. This neighborhood didn't have the streetlights on every block like hers did. Also, it was strange—most of the houses were dark, yet it was barely nine o' clock. What the heck was wrong with these people? Quiet blanketed the entire street. She reached Emily's house, and stood a minute, staring at the dark windows. Emily's parents must have been in bed already—they had to be in their 60's by now.

She walked up the driveway straight into the grass of their backyard. Their house didn't have a fence like some of the other houses did so the yard sort of bled into the trees, with the trees becoming more numerous the farther she walked into their yard. You would think they would at least have motion sensor lights back here, but the yard was as dark as the street. Had Emily wandered off and gotten lost? The forest didn't seem huge when driving by it—maybe ten miles across and only about a mile deep. Neighbors, the police, and tracking dogs had scoured the forest for days but there had been no sign of Emily. It was like she had vanished.

Jess calculated the remaining distance in her head. She would move in a straight line through the forest and could easily walk a fifteen-minute mile, faster if she wanted. Mike's house was maybe a few blocks from where she would emerge from the woods on the other side. Twenty minutes from Jake's flirty smile. The thought energized her. She paused a minute and looked over her shoulder at Emily's house. It was sad but there was nothing that would bring her back now. Jess cocked her head for any last minute advice from her mother, but the voice was silent.

The faster-than-fifteen-minute mile had not accounted for two things. One, Jess's abdomen crushing jeans made it impossible to take large strides. The material didn't give much, so jogging, or even deep breaths, were out of the question. Secondly, the twigs and assorted rocks on the forest floor were tearing up her bare feet. She'd laughed at that show where naked people tromp through the wild to survive for weeks at a time, but it didn't seem funny now.

She could either put her shoes back on and bleed more from the top of her foot or stay barefoot and risk cutting the bottom of her feet. Wearing high wedge shoes while hiking through the forest at night seemed like the stupider option—aside from cutting into her ankle, she could easily fall. Did that happen to Emily, only no one ever found her? Jess shivered in the cold night air and quickened her pace as best she could given her ensemble.

Tree branches poked her head on occasion, and

she was pretty sure she had a scratch across her forehead from one of them. Hopefully, Jake wouldn't notice. Jess made sure to go in a straight line yet there were times she had to go around a tree trunk or step out of the way of a low hanging branch. She reached up to touch her hair and pulled a leaf out of it—it no longer fell like silk over her shoulders and instead felt slightly frizzed and dirty. She kept going, trying to ignore the discomfort in her feet.

The last conversation she had with her dad popped into her head. She had found him asleep, face down at the kitchen table late one night after a double shift. She'd gently shaken him awake so he could go up to bed. Only when he raised his head, she saw he hadn't been sleeping—he'd been crying.

"Dad, are you okay?" Jess asked.

His red-rimmed eyes gazed at her. "I'm sorry."

Seeing him look so lost frightened her. She sat down next to him. "There's nothing to be sorry for."

He wiped a tear from his eye. "I know I haven't been around. It's so hard."

"It's fine. I'm fine," Jess lied. "You need some sleep."

He nodded and stood up, but then reached down to embrace Jess in an awkward hug. "You look like her, you know. You're all I have left. I don't know what I'd do if I lost you."

Jess hugged him back. "Well, I'm not going anywhere. You're stuck with me, dad."

That had been three nights ago.

Jess felt she had been walking forever—way longer than fifteen minutes. A mile sure seemed much longer in the dark. Jess pulled out her cell phone to check the time. *Ten o' clock*. It made no sense. Even with a slower than planned pace, she should have made it through to the other side long ago. Maybe she got turned around in the dark. With the way her night was going, she had turned around entirely and was heading back toward her own house.

Jess clicked on the map app to check her progress. Mike's red dot destination was not on the screen. She punched in the address again. *Location not found*. What the fresh hell was this? The five bars on her phone had dropped down to one bar. Crap. Clearly, reception in the middle of the woods wasn't great. Maybe that meant she was in the center of it and would soon be near the other side and back in cell phone range.

The temperature dropped further. The wind had stopped completely which should have been a plus, but wasn't. A deep, still cold wrapped around Jess like a blanket and made it hard to breathe, but that was probably just her body rebelling against her tight-ass jeans. She kept walking—and walking—and walking. She had to be close to the perimeter of the forest by now. She stopped to check her phone.

Eleven o'clock. Still only one bar. And now her battery light was flashing that it was low. Oh, hell no! Her phone had to hold out.

Jess looked at the sky for constellations to follow, but it was an inky black and there were so many trees. She couldn't even locate the sliver of moon she'd spotted earlier. She was exhausted and the trees seemed even denser and closer together, the foliage and branches pulled and tugged at her as she pushed through them. All she wanted at this point was a blanket and a nap. Her dad would almost be home from work.

Half past eleven. Her phone battery flashed a warning light. A light fog settled down amongst the trees making it almost impossible to see in front of her. This was not happening. The fog grew heavier; Jess's teeth chattered from the chill. Where were her shoes? She must have dropped her sandals at some point in her trek. Panic started to set in.

The fog swirled in a thick white mass. Jess's body

shook from the cold. It had to be midnight. She pulled out her phone. The screen wouldn't light up. She pushed the button again, her fingers barely able to bend from the cold. Nothing.

She started to cry. No one would find her here. Not for a long time at least. Had she told Jake or anyone that she was taking this short cut? She couldn't remember but didn't think she'd mentioned it in her texts. Jess wondered how long it took to die of hypothermia. She'd read somewhere that it was pretty peaceful—you just went to sleep and didn't wake up.

A few more steps was all Jess thought she had in her. Then she would find a nice large tree to curl up under and she would go to sleep. Maybe someone would find her—didn't cell phones have tracking ability in them? But maybe the cell phone had to be on for that to work. Her mind started to drift. She thought about her mother singing her lullabies as a child and wished she could hear her voice again.

There. A tree larger than the others rose out of the fog. That would be where she would stop and sleep. She reached the tree and touched its rough bark, walking in a slow circle around it. If she huddled down with her back to it, it might protect her from some of the chill. Her hand froze when she reached the other side of the tree.

Jess rubbed her eyes and stared. Just beyond the towering tree, the fog dissolved, leaving trailing wisps of white in the air. She took tentative steps in that direction, not quite believing her eyes. Where the fog ended was a clearing in the midst of the trees. And in the center of the clearing was a house.

The house wasn't some small cottage you'd expect to find deep in the woods. Her dad would have called this house "fancy." She'd read about some stately manor in one of her world literature classes and this house looked like what she had imagined. She had to be hallucinating from extreme exhaustion or cold, or both.

The windows were lit up from the inside as though people occupied every single room in the house. And was that music she heard? The faint notes of classical music drifted through the air. Like Mozart or one of those other old guys she'd heard in her music elective.

Jess approached the massive front door. It was made out of a heavy, dark wood, with an ornate copper doorknocker. Who had door-knockers? She heard people inside the home. Many people talking and laughing. The classical music was louder and sounded like live instruments. It sure wasn't Mike's house, but it definitely sounded like a party.

Someone in there had to have a cell phone. She wasn't going to die of the cold. This made her so happy. She no longer cared about Mike's stupid party—or Jake. Let some other girl have him. She just wanted to go home.

She lifted the metal door knocker and tapped it against the door. No response. She raised it again and slammed it down several times. They probably couldn't hear her over the music. Still no answer.

Jess couldn't wait any longer. She needed to get out of the cold. Surely, they would understand if she came inside. She twisted the knob and tested the door. It opened with a slight creaking sound.

"Hello?" Jess took a step inside.

The warmth of the home embraced her. Oh wow, it felt amazing to be out of the cold, night air. As soon as Jess closed the door behind her, the chill was like a distant memory. Jess stood in an immense entry area and stared in awe at the chandelier above her, which glittered with thousands of crystals adorning four gargoyles that leaped from the center. The staircase curved up behind it to another floor. An arched doorway was to her right, and through couples in elegant clothes danced across the floor of a grand ballroom. An orchestra played in the back of the room.

The music grew louder as Jess approached. She hid behind the doorframe and peeked her head around it to survey the room. Tables on the side of the room were piled high with food making her mouth water. Not that she could eat much, if anything, in these jeans. She looked down, self-conscious. Her right foot was covered in crusted blood, her jeans were streaked with dirt, and many of the sequins on her tank top had been plucked off by tree branches and were dangling sadly around her chest. She didn't even want to know what her hair and face looked like.

The party guests were all dressed in 18th century clothes—the woman in elaborate corseted gowns and the men with ruffles down the front of their shirts. Several of the woman carried intricate lace fans and paused from the dancing at times to fan themselves. Many of the men wore powdered wigs. It had to be a theme party—adults loved those things. They moved in pair to what looked like a waltz she'd seen on some reality dance show. One man bowed down and kissed the gloved hand of his partner at the end of a song.

Not a one of them noticed her hiding behind the

doorway. If she could find someone to help her, she would be on her way. Her dad would be worried sick about her by now. Maybe she could borrow a phone and call him. Or maybe someone had a charger for her phone. She pulled it out but the screen stayed dark and still wouldn't turn on.

Jess decided to try another part of the house. With a party this big, there had to be hired help, and they might be less likely to care what she looked like. She would try to find the kitchen. Ornate wall sconces lit the dark paneled hallway.

She followed the scent of roasted meat wafting through the house, but stopped at a doorway. It was a study with book-lined shelves and a fire roaring in a stone fireplace on the far wall. Just in front of the fireplace was a plush sofa with a blanket draped over the back of it. The temptation was too strong. She would get to the kitchen soon enough.

Jess stepped into the room. "Hello? Anyone here?"

No one answered so she crept over to the sofa, letting the warmth from the fire wash over her. A plate of luscious strawberries sat on an antique end table. Jess didn't want to be rude but no one would miss one or two pieces of fruit. She lifted one to her mouth. It was the sweetest strawberry she'd ever tasted. She wanted another but was so very tired. Jess touched the soft blanket; it felt like a cloud. She wrapped it around her and curled up on the couch, her head resting closest to the fire. Just a short nap. She closed her eyes.

A COLD HAND touched Jess's shoulder from behind and she woke with a start, a scream tearing from her throat.

"I'm sorry, I didn't mean to startle you."

Jess sat up and blinked. Where was she? It took a minute before it all came back to her—Mike's party, the forest, getting lost, and finding this house.

She turned around and gasped. Though stunning was not a word she would have ever used to describe a guy, that was the word that came to her. He had long, golden hair pulled back behind his neck in a ponytail and piercing blue eyes. She couldn't figure out his age—he was dressed in a dark suit that looked like it was on trend for the year 1800.

Jess tucked a wild tuft of hair behind her ear. She was a hot mess. "I'm . . . I'm so sorry for coming into your house, but I was lost in the woods and it's freezing out tonight, and I was walking for so long, and my feet were killing me, and I . . . I need help."

He smiled and something about his straight white teeth and full lips made Jess's heart race. "Of course. You look in need of some assistance." He stared at her a minute, then offered his hand to help her up from the sofa. "I'm Jeremy."

"Jeremy," she murmured. "I'm Jess."

"Welcome to my home. Let us get you cleaned up."

The man kept his hand at her elbow, gently guiding her through the halls of his home, giving her a tour of the various rooms along the way. They passed a conservatory, a library, and a sitting room. His grasp on her arm was quite proper but there was a firm pressure that Jess found unsettling. What did he do for a living to have a home like this?

The smell of roasted meats grew strong. And Jess's mouth watered. She swallowed as they stood in the doorway. "This, of course, is the kitchen where my staff prepares all of food for gatherings."

"How often do you have these parties?" Jess asked. Seemed like a truck load of work for one night.

He smiled. "Why, every night, of course."

Jess gasped. Not only was that a ton of party

planning, but how did all the guests have that much free time on their hands?

Her eyes drifted back to the food. Several cooks were placing giant turkey legs on silver platters, while another piled a tray with assorted cheeses and grapes. Jeremy had started to move on but Jess couldn't move, her eyes fixed on the feast in front of her.

"Oh, where are my manners? You must be famished." Jeremy spoke to one of the staff and then gestured at Jess. "This way, *mademoiselle.*"

Jess wasn't sure what he had just called her but she loved the sound it made coming out of his mouth. She followed him numbly to a private dining room where an intimate table was set for two. China place settings, cloth napkins, polished silverware and crystal goblets adorned a table covered by a silk tablecloth. Several candles glowed softly in the center. Jeremy pulled out the chair for Jess. She sat down as he took the chair opposite her. She was certain that no one had ever been this nice to her.

A waiter came in with a plate full of meats, fruits, and cheeses and placed it in front of Jess. She grabbed a turkey leg and ripped into it without thinking. The skin was crisped to perfection, and the meat melted in her mouth. She'd never tasted food this good and hoped her jeans wouldn't bust open. As she gulped down a mouthful, she was aware of Jeremy watching her. He had no food in front of him.

She wiped her mouth with the napkin. "Sorry, I'm really hungry. You're not eating?"

She chewed off another mouthful of turkey before he could respond.

Jeremy smiled, and it struck Jess that his canine teeth were very long—almost wolf-like. "Eat all you like. I've already dined but would like to keep you company if you don't mind."

Jess shook her head; her mouth was too full to answer. She didn't mind at all. This guy could stay around as much as he liked. She popped a plump purple grape into her mouth, and the sweetness exploded on her tongue. There was something she wanted to ask—she needed help with something—but she couldn't remember what it was. She was sure it would come to her, so she kept eating while Jeremy watched her.

Her stomach finally full, Jess placed her napkin on the table. She hoped she hadn't looked like a total pig but the meal had been amazing—so good that Jess had stopped trying to calculate the total calories mid-meal. The button of her jeans threatened to pop off any second.

"Thank you," she said. "That was delicious. You could totally start your own restaurant—the chefs are super talented."

He smiled. "You're welcome. Now, how about a warm shower and something more suitable to wear."

Jess's cheeks grew warm in embarrassment at her tattered top and dirty jeans. She knew there was a reason she looked so awful. What was it?

They went up a spiral, dark wooden staircase--only slightly less grand than the one she'd seen at the front of the house—and down a small hallway.

"I think this chamber should suit you." Jeremy opened the door to the room.

Jess loved how he said chamber instead of bedroom. He was really staying in character with the whole theme. One had to admire his commitment to the part. She blushed when he caught her staring.

"After you." Jeremy waved her into the room.

A white four-poster bed sat in the center of the room. Pale gauzy side panels flowed from the top to the pillow-y mattress. It was a bed fit for a princess. Whoever lived in this room was the luckiest girl in the world. A large bay window held a bench seat with satin throw pillows. Everything was majestic.

Jeremy strode over to a large wardrobe. He pulled the double doors open at the same time. "I'm sure there's something in here that will suit you." He considered the options in front of him, then pulled out a floor-length red velvet dress.

He held it up to Jess in front of a free-standing antique mirror next to the dresser. "What do you think? This is a very flattering shade for you, I do think."

Jess had to admit that the color suited her, and the dress was gorgeous. The only theme-party she'd been to before had been a sock hop, and she'd thought poodle skirts were the worst thing ever. How was a boy supposed to see your legs in a skirt that reached your ankles?

Attached to the chamber was a bathroom with an old-fashioned claw foot tub that had a shower at one end of it and a lace curtain encircling the whole thing. It was the focal point of the room. A nearby vanity with a small stool in front of it contained a mirror and an assortment of lotions, perfumes, and make-up.

Jeremy gestured toward the tub. "You will find everything you need in there. I will wait for you downstairs by the ballroom." He bowed and backed out of the bathroom.

The thought of getting naked and bathing in a strange house with random people should have bothered her, but Jess found it hard to muster any worry. She felt so safe and at home here. She'd never used a bathroom this nice, and she wasn't about to skip it.

She waited until the water was steaming hot before she stepped in. The shampoo smelled of honeysuckle as she massaged her hair into a rich lather. She already hoped she could come back to this house again—surely there was an easier way to access it from the other side of the forest. She hadn't seen Jeremy around school before. Maybe he was in college? Did he have a girlfriend? The name of another boy she'd liked tickled her mind, but she could not remember it for the life of her.

The soap smelled of roses and her skin felt soft and smooth when she rinsed herself. She could stay there for hours. The thought of Jeremy waiting for her downstairs made her turn off the water. What if he asked her to dance? She had no idea how to ballroom dance but suspected he would gently lead her, and it would be magical.

She grabbed a fluffy towel and dried off, then wrapped it around herself and sat down at the vanity. The lotions alone must have cost a fortune. She didn't recognize the names on anything, but they all sounded like fancy brands. She used a large round brush to pull her air into smooth waves as it dried. Jess marveled at the choices in eye shadows, lipsticks and blushes which also looked expensive.

It was a guest bedroom that was always ready for the next visitor. Like a bed-and-breakfast. That must be what this place was. It would certainly explain all the old, antique-looking stuff here. She would have to ask Jeremy about that. Oh, and she remembered she needed a phone but wasn't sure why.

Where was her phone? She looked around for the clothes she'd discarded on the floor before bathing but didn't see her jeans or tank anywhere. Shoot—her phone had been in the pocket of her jeans. Had someone come in while she was in the tub and taken her clothes? Jeremy probably had staff come in to get them so they could clean them for her. He was such a gentleman like that.

As she finished her hair and make-up, a weird sense of déjà vu passed over her. Like she had just done all this not long ago. Oh right, she'd gotten ready for the party at her classmate's house. What was his name? Jess yawned. It must be the middle of the night because it had been close to midnight the last time she'd checked her phone. Who knew 18th century parties were so wild?

Jess went back into the chamber—she liked the

sound of that word—and slid into the soft dress. It seemed made for her. The material skimmed her body and dipped down enough in the chest to be a bit risqué but not enough that it crossed the line into trashy. It was floor length, and though it didn't show off her fit legs, it clung to her form in a way that she bet Jeremy would notice.

A pair of red heels sat on the floor by the mirror. She tentatively pulled them on, but the straps didn't touch the blisters on her ankle. She leaned down. A faint red mark showed where her sandal had rubbed her earlier, but it looked much better after the shower. The rose soap might have had aloe in it. Jess's mom had told her aloe had healing properties after Jess stayed out in the sun too long one day and her mother had spread an aloe gel on her shoulders in soothing strokes.

Jess stood in front of the mirror and twirled in a slow circle, admiring herself in the mirror. Her mother would approve though she'd argue that Jess looked too old for her age in this dress. A pair of diamond drop earrings on a small table caught her eye. Surely, they were meant for this dress. She put the earrings on and loved how they caught the light. She had to tell everyone about this bed-and-breakfast—this place would be the hit of the town.

The music still played as Jess stepped into the hallway. She followed the sound and walked back down the curved staircase, through the long corridor toward the ballroom. Jeremy stood leaning against the doorway, waiting for her.

He bowed when she reached him. "You look extraordinary, *mademoiselle*."

Jess blushed. "Thank you. This dress is gorgeous."

He smiled. "Clothing only brings out the beauty of its wearer." He offered his arm to her. "Shall we?"

She took his arm. "We shall."

They entered the ballroom and every head swiveled in their direction. She saw several people nodding their heads, as though in approval. Jess was really glad she hadn't come in here earlier when she'd been a wreck. Still others bowed slightly in deference to Jeremy as he passed. A gentleman with power. Jess liked that in a guy.

He led her to the dance floor and several couples cleared some space. The orchestra began a new song, and Jeremy took her hand and instructed her to follow his lead. She had no problem with that because this was nothing like the moves she and her friends did at school dances. Jess felt as though she were gliding on air as he expertly twirled and guided her around the room. When one of his hands moved to her waist, her heart thudded. She dared to raise her eyes to his, and he stared with such intensity that she blushed again.

"I've been waiting for one like you for a long time," he murmured.

What did that mean? The music changed while they danced and danced, staring into one another's eyes. When the next number ended, she forced herself to pull her gaze from his. She looked up at the gold gilded ceiling, painted with beautiful intricate scenes of gods and goddesses. Numerous wall sconces gleamed on the walls but Jess noted there were no clocks. She yawned again.

"What time is it, Jeremy?" she asked. "These parties sure go late."

He reached down to hold her hand. His fingers caressed her wrist in a way that felt intimate yet also unsettling. "My parties don't start until midnight and they go all night long." He raised her hand and kissed it gently. "Don't worry. You'll get used to it, *mademoiselle.*"

The feel of his lips on her skin thrilled her. She loved that he planned to invite her back to another party, yet something bothered her. Her name. She was positive she'd told him her name but, he'd never said it. Not that she didn't love his French words, but it felt almost like—well, like she could be anyone. He could call anyone that.

Jess looked around the room but didn't see anyone holding a phone. How could that be? Or maybe it was a requirement of the theme party so that you got the full nineteenth century experience. Surely, Jeremy would have a phone she could use, which reminded her that she needed to get her phone back.

An older man in a staff uniform appeared by Jeremy's side and whispered something into his ear. Jeremy nodded. "I will be right back. Why don't you get yourself some refreshments?"

"Wait, I need to ask you—" Jess stopped.

A question had been on the tip of her tongue a second ago. What was it? Jess knew it was important. Like really important.

Jeremy kissed her hand. "I'm sure you will think of it. I will return in a moment."

With that, he departed with the man. Jess stood in the center of the floor as couples continued to dance around her. Feeling a little numb, she walked to the long tables filled with food and drink. She picked up a glass of punch—it smelled fruity—and gulped it down, not realizing how thirsty she'd been.

Must have been all the dancing. She grabbed a second glass and wandered down the length of the table to see all the varied appetizers.

"Isn't this a grand time?" a woman asked her. She patted her platinum hair before placing several strawberries on her plate. "Jeremy has the most divine parties." She surveyed Jess and smiled. "You are such a lucky girl. It's been years since he chose one like you."

Jess frowned. "What do you mean?"

The woman's eyes widened. "Hmmm. What do I mean? It's . . . well, most of us here are guests and staff. I don't know how he decides the others . . ." She trailed off, looking confused.

What on earth was she talking about? Were there nineteenth century drugs at this party? The woman handed Jess a strawberry and Jess tried to formulate her thoughts. There was so much she needed to know.

"How long have you known Jeremy and been coming to these parties?" Jess asked, taking a small bite of the berry.

Strawberry seeds dotted the woman's teeth as she smiled widely in response. "For ages and ages." She frowned. "It's like I never leave. I live on the grounds . . . we all do. There are many rooms here."

She stared at Jess a minute, then looked around the ballroom and spoke again, but more to herself. "Why don't I leave?"

Jess needed her help. But with what? She couldn't think straight.

"Excuse me, dear, I have to return to my suitor. You know how they get when you're gone too long." She winked and walked away before Jess could ask any more.

Nobody used the word suitor. This was the most elaborate theme party she'd ever heard about—they took it so seriously. It was like the party version of people who did those Civil War reenactments.

Toward the end of the table Jess noticed platters of desserts. She had stuffed herself full of dinner, but there was always room for a little dessert. Her eyes widened at all the choices. Plates of tiny teacakes, bowls of pudding, and trays of what she thought her mom called *petits fours*. One serving platter was empty. Jess surveyed the sweets, deciding which one to try first.

A serving woman appeared to replace the empty tray with a fresh one brimming with dark and milk chocolates. Just in time. Chocolate was always a good option. Jess reached for one before the woman had even taken her hands away. "These look fabulous."

The woman studied her but did not respond. Middle-aged, with pale watery blue eyes, her hair had the light greyish tone of someone who was once blond. Something was familiar about her, but Jess couldn't place her. Maybe she was a neighbor or the parent of a classmate. The woman glanced at Jess's dress and an expression of sadness flitted across her face. She sighed. "Ah, I remember that dress."

Jess's mouth was full of chocolate. Before she could ask what the woman was talking about, she had disappeared back into the crowd. She tried to clear her head. There was something she needed to do, something she needed help with, but her thoughts wouldn't form. It was the middle of the night, and her brain was fried with exhaustion.

She just needed a good night's sleep in her bed to feel better. Her bed. She thought of the room upstairs. That wasn't her bed. Was it? Jess tried to picture another bed—her own bedroom—but nothing came. *Run.* Who said that? The voice in her head was familiar to her, a female voice, but Jess couldn't place it. Yet somehow, she knew it was a voice she trusted.

"There you are, *mademoiselle*. Here, you must try

one of the cherry-filled dark chocolates. They are heavenly." Jeremy placed the chocolate to her lips.

Jess wanted to protest. She had been about to go somewhere—she was positive she'd been about to run somewhere—but where? His blue gaze made her insides mushy. She parted her lips, and he put the chocolate in her mouth. She bit down and sweet cherry liquid ran over her tongue, mixing with the richness of the chocolate. It was delectable. Jess wanted more. He placed the rest of the chocolate in her mouth, and his finger grazed her tongue. An electric current ran through her. She forgot all about going anywhere—who would ever want to run from this man?

"You seemed a little upset before. Are you feeling better? Did you remember what you wanted to inquire about?" Concern etched Jeremy's eyes.

The last bit of chocolate slid down her throat. She couldn't think of a time she had ever felt better. There was only one question she wanted to ask him as she looped her arm through his. "Shall we dance?"

JESS STRETCHED her arms overhead as dappled

sunlight filtered through the windows of her bedroom. She lounged amongst the pillows on her bed and thought about how lucky she was. Wasn't she? I mean, she was lonely most days because Jeremy wasn't there, but he always came home at midnight for the parties. Every night. She didn't know how he had the energy for it but he managed. Every once in a while, fear crept into the edges of Jess's mind but she knew she was being silly. What was there to be afraid of in a place like this?

Guests filled many of the rooms inside the mansion, yet they never ventured out during the day. Jess only saw them at the night parties. She often spotted staff delivering food to their rooms but they seemed content to stay there. Jess had long ago stopped wondering what they did all day long.

Jess parted the sheers of her four-poster bed and slid her feet into soft slippers. The smell of bacon and eggs drifted into her room, making her mouth water. Breakfast was the most important meal of the day after all. Someone had told her that once though she couldn't remember who. She wrapped her silk robe around her and ventured down to the kitchen.

A place had been set for her in the small dining room, with a crystal goblet of orange juice by her food. She sat down to eat like she had for the past few weeks but just before she brought the forkful of fluffy eggs to her mouth, a woman ran in the room.

"Stop! Don't eat." The woman had pale watery eyes and longish grey hair. Jess had seen her around the estate. She seemed frantic. "I've been under the weather and couldn't eat this morning, and now I'm starting to remember."

Jess froze mid-forkful. "Is something wrong with the eggs?"

The woman looked around, as though afraid. She stepped closer to the table and spoke in a low voice. "What's your name?"

"My name is . . ." A frown crossed her face. What *was* her name? All she could think of was *mademoiselle* but that didn't seem right. "That's strange. Give me a second—my name is . . ." She grew frustrated and slammed her fork down. "Why? What's *your* name?"

The woman shook her head. Up close, she looked younger than Jess had thought; closer to 50 than in her 60's—the grey hair made her look older than she was. "I don't know. I remembered once, years ago . . . I think . . . I can't be certain." She peered at the plate of eggs in front of Jess. "It must be the food."

"What, like the food is enchanted or something?"

Jess laughed. "That's something straight out of a fairytale. Give me a break." Still, why couldn't she remember her own name? That seemed an odd thing to forget.

The woman backed toward the door. "I will forget that I ever told you this. Look at the portrait inside Jeremy's wing. He's not who you think. I tried to get away once but it's all so hazy." She put her fingers to her temples and rubbed. "There's something else. Do you see what I've become?" She gestured at her drab staff attire. "You will be me someday. He's cursed, you're cursed, we're all cursed." Her eyes had a faraway look in them and her next words came out in a sing-song voice.

> *"The time you first meet him determines your fate,*
> > *you were quite lucky you arrived here so late,*
> > *because the girl before me,*
> > *who arrived at mid-day—he ate."*

Revulsion roiled Jess's stomach. Why would she be told such hideous stories while she was trying to enjoy breakfast? And she would never be like that woman—Jess was Jeremy's girlfriend, not some random servant. After all, she was the sole focus of

Jeremy's attention every night. Everyone saw that. That had to mean something.

The old woman shook her head as though trying to clear it. "I'm forgetting again, I have to go." She backed out of the room but leaned in one last time. "Remember, don't eat."

Jess stared at her eggs that were growing cold. What an odd woman. She would have to ask Jeremy about her when he returned. Her stomach growled but a nagging worry wouldn't let her pick up the fork. She'd never been in Jeremy's wing of the manor before—he'd never told her not to go there—she'd just never had the thought that she should.

The sun rose in the sky, and she noted the brilliant blue color as she gazed out the dining room window. Majestic trees surrounded the estate on all sides. It was so beautiful here. At some point, she would have to venture outside and get some fresh air but the thought rarely occurred to her. She rose from her seat and headed toward the door. She would check out the portrait, and then she would have staff make her a fresh plate of breakfast.

Jeremy's wing was on the far side of the estate. She wandered through the halls, admiring the tapestries on the walls. Odd that she hadn't had the urge to do this before. A set of carved wooden doors were at the end of the final corridor. Though she knew Jeremy was out of town, she hesitated and knocked lightly. "Hello?"

When no one responded, she pushed open the doors. They swung silently, and she entered the grand room. Jeremy's room made her own expansive guest suite seem tiny. A golden duvet covered a king-sized bed, and there were floor-to-ceiling windows along one exterior wall. A fireplace, couch, and table with books were near the windows. The magnificence of his quarters was awe-inspiring. She stared back at the bed again and blushed, as though she had a fleeting memory of being there before. But that was impossible, as she'd never been in this wing. Jeremy had certainly visited her room many times though. She flushed again.

Why had she come here? She turned in a circle to look around when her eyes caught a back corner of the room, in a dark recess where the light from the windows did not reach. The area was hidden by a long heavy curtain. Hmmm . . . interesting. She crept to the curtain and had a sudden thought that she had no desire to look back there. That she should leave.

She'd come all this way and Jeremy would be back from his trip soon, so she might not get another chance. She swept the curtain aside and stepped into the small recess. It was very dark with nothing but a tiny table with an oil lamp on it. She turned up the lamp, and a wide smile lit her face. A large portrait of Jeremy hung on the wall. His blond hair fell around his shoulders instead of being pulled back, and he was dressed in fine clothes. Looking at him always made her heart beat faster. She leaned closer and saw a small inscription at the bottom right corner of the painting. She squinted her eyes. *Dusk*. That was it. What did that mean?

Oh well, it was a very nice portrait, though she didn't know why she had felt compelled to come see it. She would be sure to compliment Jeremy on it the next time she saw him. She turned to leave and saw a second portrait on the wall to her right. Her eyes widened. The word wouldn't come to her at first to describe what she was seeing. A grotesque creature with red glowing eyes and sharp pointed teeth stared at her. Demon. The word was demon. Something about the eyes was familiar. Despite her horror, she leaned closer, not understanding why she felt she knew him. Her eyes fell on the inscription at the bottom of the portrait. *Dawn*.

And a third inscription evenly spaced between the two portraits:

The time you first meet him determines your fate.

She recoiled in terror. No. She backed out of the curtain, walking backwards toward the door.

A growl erupted behind her. She whirled around and screamed. The demon stood there as though he'd just stepped out of the portrait. More animal than human, with long, deadly teeth and matted fur covering its hulking body. She searched desperately for some part of Jeremy in the creature but even the eyes were dark pools of red.

A scream ripped from her throat. *Run.* She darted toward the doorway.

She tore down the hall and the thing chased after her, its claw catching the back of her robe once and tearing it. She raced down the corridors, not daring to look behind her, and leapt down the curved stairwell three stairs at a time. The creature's ragged breathing seemed almost on top of her. Finally, the large front door to the house came into view as she careened around the corner. If only she could make it outside.

Twenty more feet. Her legs burned as she ran for her life. A guttural angry growl erupted behind her, and she lunged for the doorknob. She cranked it open as she felt something slice through her leg. Just then, a woman screamed from behind her, as though to get the demon's attention.

She flew out of the house and into the woods, which were shrouded in fog despite the daylight. She sprinted until her lungs were about to burst, and she realized the fog had cleared. Blazing sunlight almost blinded her despite the thick trees and she stumbled over a tree root and fell.

She blinked as she stared down at herself. What the hell was she wearing? A silk rose-colored bathrobe that looked like it came from the 18th century. Blood ran down the back of her leg and she noticed a large gash down her right calf. Now that the adrenaline had slowed in her body, the pain was evident. Had she been cut by a tree branch while running? She looked around and shook her head. Where was she?

It was some kind of forest but she had no memory of why she was here. Wait. A party. That's it! She had been headed to a party and took a short cut through the woods. It had been so cold during the night and she'd been convinced she would die of hypothermia. She must have fallen asleep and somehow survived.

Her dad. She had to get home. He must be going out of his mind. She could picture him as she walked in the door. "Jess!" he'd exclaim and then embrace her in a bear hug. Jess. For some reason, her own name brought her an immense source of relief.

Jess pushed herself up from the ground, dabbed at her wound with the robe, and started walking. Sam had been right. These woods were messed up. She should never have come this way. She'd even be okay with Sam telling her, "I told you so."

Jess reached for her phone and froze. If she'd fallen asleep in the woods on the way to the party, then why was she wearing this crazy robe? The pockets were empty, her phone nowhere to be found. A horrifying thought dawned on her. She'd heard about those drugs that could be slipped in your drink and caused total memory loss—date rape drugs.

What if Jess had been drugged at the party? It was the only thing she could think of that would explain her memory loss and missing clothes. Jess started to cry. She wanted to go home. Her dad would help her figure out what to do. Everything would be okay.

The sunlight warmed her, but her eyes were super sensitive to the light. Like she hadn't seen the sun in weeks which made no sense. She kept walking away from the direction of the fog. It's not like fog could hurt her, but she felt safer moving as far away as possible. She stepped carefully through the roots with her bare feet.

Her stomach growled, and she thought of breakfast. Jess decided to throw her diet out the window and scarf down some of her dad's Froot Loops when she got home. Or was it lunchtime? She looked up but couldn't see the location of the sun through the trees. She would have to wait until the trees thinned and she had a better view.

After a while, Jess grew tired. This forest was bigger than she'd realized. She should almost be at the edge by now. The shadows from the trees grew longer. It had to be close to dinner time now. Maybe she would rest a minute and then keep going.

Jess sat down a minute and leaned against a tree. She was beyond hungry and totally exhausted but did not want to be stuck in the forest once the sun went down. The bitter cold was not something she wanted to go through again. She would give anything to have her phone.

A raindrop hit Jess's face. *Wake up!* She opened her eyes. "Mom?"

Jess fully woke up and looked around at the inky blackness. No! She'd fallen asleep and now it was night again. She had no idea how late it was but it was cold. And drizzling. A crack of thunder sounded overhead and the sky opened up.

The torrential downpour came out of nowhere. Jess pulled herself to her feet and ran. The trees shielded her from some of the rain but she was still drenched within minutes, her bathrobe soaked and clinging to her goose-pimpled skin. She no longer had any idea the direction she was going and kept having to push her wet hair out of her eyes.

Jess was not going to spend the night in the woods again. She was determined to get out of the frickin' forest. A cloud of fog enveloped her, and a sense of dread overcame her. The fog was bad. She couldn't say why, but it was. She had to get out of there. Jess pushed through the fog blindly, feeling her way around trees, until a few minutes later when she breathed a sigh of relief. No fog.

What was that? Bright light emerged from the darkness like a beacon. Jess rounded a tree and a mansion loomed before her. It looked familiar . . . but maybe that was because it seemed straight out of a fairy tale. She took a few hesitant steps toward the house as rain continued to pelt her. The door opened wide. Jess blinked and held her hand up to shield her face from the rain.

An old woman stood in the doorway illuminated

by the lights within the house. Jess drew closer, shivering in her robe. Behind the woman stood the most beautiful blond man she'd ever seen. Jess couldn't help feeling excitement beneath the cold and hunger.

The woman held a tray of large strawberries in her hands. She held them out toward Jess as Jess walked up to the door. "Here dear, come in out of this awful storm and have something to eat."

"Yes, do come in," said the beautiful man.

Jess smiled. She was saved. She would make it after all.

She picked out a strawberry and disappeared into the house.

A NOTE FROM KRISTI HELVIG

This story is partly based on a darker version of Beauty and the Beast that came to me in a dream after I saw my daughter perform in the play at school. Mixed with this was an incident involving our son's baseball tournament in a neighboring town. The baseball field was within a normal-looking suburban subdivision, except that it was surrounded by a forest, and many of the houses in the neighborhood had hexes painted above the front doors. Intrigued, I asked around and someone told me there was a legend that the hexes for warding off a demon that supposedly lived in the woods. As a total sucker for urban legends, it was all this writer needed to hear to know that the forest was going to tie in with my Beauty and the Beast story.

Thank you for reading THE MISSING. Here's a sneak peek at my paranormal thriller, THE WING COLLECTOR...

THE WING COLLECTOR

"*Trifle not with humans and their greedy, selfish ways; By remaining strong and Pure, we will end their wicked days.*"
        —Book of Faery

DEAD THINGS

Epping Forest, England
August 27, 6:04 a.m.

I WAIT for her behind a large oak tree. Cool mist dampens the morning air, yet I feel no chill. I'm too focused. I know how it will unfold; the girl's initial confusion will give way to anger, then fear. Despite what I am about to do, I don't want her scared.

I want her dead.

Killing her is necessary in order to find the One.

Streaks of gold penetrate the woods, and I watch the rising sun with impatience. The less light, the better.

Light, tentative footsteps crunch the dead leaves underfoot. The girl mumbles under her breath, "I don't know why we had to meet so early."

I take a slight step in her direction and a twig snaps.

She peers into the fog. "Matt?" she whispers. "Matt, is that you?"

I step out from behind the tree. "My deepest apologies, but Matt couldn't make it."

She starts to run when she sees the knife, and the crumpled note from her crush—as written by yours truly—slips from her hand. Turning her back to me only makes what I have to do easier.

I WIPE the blood on a cloth that I'll later burn. One down, but many remain. I won't waver. I won't tire.

I'll make the world a better place—one freak at a time.

CAROLINA DREAMING
Chapel Hill, North Carolina
August 27, 1:04 a.m.

THE SCREAM TORE from my throat as I jerked awake, certain someone was in the room with me. Shaking, I bolted upright in bed, the sheets drenched in sweat. I fumbled in the dark for the waste basket and vomited into it. The room was almost pitch-black thanks to the thick, custom-made shutters that covered the inside of all windows in the house.

"Lila!"

Light flooded the room and I shielded my eyes from the glare. Mom ran to my bed and pushed the hair back from my face. She stared with concern at the stench-filled waste basket. "Lila, what's wrong? Are you okay?"

I couldn't stop shaking. "I don't know." Had I had a nightmare? My eyes fell on the large rose-quartz crystal in her other hand. "Seriously, is that your idea of a weapon?"

Mom managed a weak smile, her blond hair in frizzed ringlets around her face. "It was the closest thing. She pressed the back of her hand to my forehead. "No fever . . . you're just clammy."

I clutched my blanket around me. "I thought it was impossible for me to get sick."

Her brow wrinkled. "I thought that too. Was it a bad dream?"

I tried, and failed, to grasp at something at the edges of my memory. I shook my head. "I don't know. I can't remember."

Just to be sure, she checked my closet and under my bed with the crystal raised above her head like some kind of hippie warrior. Satisfied that no one lurked inside my room, she pocketed the rose quartz. "I'm worried about you. Do you want me to stay?"

"No, I'm fine, really." For emphasis, I leaned back against my pillow and tugged the blanket up to my chin.

"Okay, but yell if you need anything." She took the waste basket and lingered a minute by the doorway, concern etched across her face, before she flicked off the light and returned to her room.

The darkness fell heavy around me, enveloping me in a black cocoon. Only the lazy whirring of the ceiling fan overhead masked the silence. I tried to steady my rapid breathing. No one was here in the house aside from Mom and me, same as always. We were safe. I told myself this over and over again for the next few hours until sunrise . . . because I couldn't quite make myself believe it.

TICK TOCK

Heathrow Airport, London

August 30

I BUCKLE INTO MY SEAT, ignoring the chipper flight attendant who acts as if the life vest under the seat can actually prevent death if the plane plummets into the icy Atlantic. Still, a smile creeps across my face at what I've accomplished . . . at what is waiting for me across the pond. I can almost smell them— their rotten souls permeating the air around me. I don't know why they think they have the right to be here at all. Like they can fool us into thinking they are human. That the hideousness behind their normal-looking exteriors will go undetected for long. Stupid creatures.

The plane lifts into the air and I settle back in my

seat, gazing at the splendid morning sky out my window. The countdown has begun, and I am the timekeeper. They think they are better than humans, but I'll show them just how wrong they are.

PATIENCE AND OTHER WASTED VIRTUES

September 27

2:13 p.m.

IT TAKES me almost a month to find the next one. The pace will have to pick up if I have any hope of succeeding. The waiting is the hardest part—double checking their sub-human status, planning the most effective location for their death, and in this case, neglecting my regular obligations in order to finish the task. No one will notice, though—I've covered my tracks too well.

She makes the mistake of leaving early today. Maybe she senses something is wrong, senses that I'm near. Sadly, in trying to save herself, she leaves herself vulnerable—walking home alone by a creek. Tsk, tsk. And to think they consider themselves smarter than humans.

Such pretty wings, though. I have plans for these.

My glee is barely contained as her blood soaks into the water . . . as her life ebbs to nothingness. Not just because I've taken out another one, but because I feel closer to . . . The One.

Of all the mutants I will kill, none will compare to the One.

VOMIT REVISITED
September 27
2:13 p.m.

THE WAY THEY STARED, you'd think they had never seen a girl run before. More likely, it was that they'd never seen *me* run. Maybe the quiet girl charging through school as if her life depended on it did warrant some attention. Still, I didn't appreciate the amusement I saw on their faces. Or the laughter. Though I had no idea what was happening to me, it felt like death was a distinct possibility.

"What's up, Kincade, they givin' away free calculators in class today?" one boy yelled.

Ignoring him, I raced down the hallway, my footsteps echoing against the tile. The wrenching sensation in my stomach increased, propelling me faster. I threw open the girls' restroom door and darted inside. My gut lurched as I locked the stall.

What the hell is going on? Sweat beaded on my forehead. Bending over with my head hovering over the toilet, I focused on the cracked floor tiles as I gagged, a stream of bile erupting from my mouth. *Gross.* Maybe it was the eggs I had for breakfast; maybe they'd gone bad. The irony wasn't lost on me that I might have kept myself safe all these years, only to die of food poisoning.

Get a grip, Lila. I'd heard about the flu—had even seen one of my classmates puke—but I'd never experienced it for myself. I was supposed to be immune to illness—one of the few perks of being me—yet I'd puked twice in as many months. Though it was still difficult to muster much empathy for most of my classmates, I had to admit this sucked.

At the sound of the homeroom bell, I attempted to stand. I put a hand on each side of the stall, partially covering a scribble proclaiming *Lexie was here.* Different colored writing underneath inquired, *Where hasn't she been?*

Relief washed over me as the wave of sickness passed. I stumbled to the sink and splashed cold water on my face, then reached over my shoulders to make sure the bindings hadn't slipped. As much as I hadn't wanted my "extra parts" discovered, not vomiting in the hallway of Northeast High had taken priority. The wayward hair staring back at me from the mirror would have to wait. Only one more class to go. I hurried out the door toward my locker.

THE BELL SIGNALED the start of Ms. Gable's Advanced Algebra, or AA, as nerds like me called it. It was my absolute favorite class. I pressed my fingertip against the pencil point to ensure adequate sharpness, a satisfied smile on my lips. Some girls might be obsessed with boys or shoes, but my obsession involved numbers. *Why shop when you could find the unknown variable in a complex equation?*

Although my classmates complained that algebra had little value in the real world, they didn't have a clue. There was inherent perfection in numbers. Something was either right or wrong—no pesky shades of gray.

I shifted in my seat, my bindings already damp from the humidity still hanging in the warm autumn air. It was marginally better than the thick heat of August—North Carolina summers were brutal, and wreaked havoc on both my hair and my bindings. When I looked up toward the front of the classroom, the empty teacher's desk stared back. Weird. Ms. Gable was never late.

Giggling erupted behind me.

"Seriously, did you see Jackie's pants? I mean could her ass look any bigger?"

Miranda. Miranda thought anyone weighing over a hundred pounds belonged on laxatives.

"Speaking of the fashion-challenged . . . ," Miranda continued, then thankfully dropped her voice to a whisper.

Even though I could no longer hear her remarks, when Glen, the big football jock with an even bigger mouth, laughed the loudest, I knew who they were talking about. He never let an opportunity pass if it involved harassing me. His voice echoed through the classroom. "What a nerd."

What a jerk, I wanted to say, but didn't—I never did. Instead, I shrank in my seat, cheeks burning. My ever-present hoodie was a precautionary measure rather than a lack of fashion sense, but Miranda couldn't know that.

Trendy tops didn't provide adequate wing coverage.

I spotted Ms. Gable outside the classroom

speaking to the assistant principal, Mr. Turner. Or maybe flirting, judging by the way she flipped her hair. *Great.* This gave everyone more time to dissect my fashion faux pas. All I wanted was to tackle another formula—insert more numbers into their proper place.

"Seriously, I'm dying here. My mouth tastes like twice-baked cardboard. Anyone got any gum?" asked a boy in the back of the room.

Miranda giggled. "Ash, Ms. Gable will just make you spit it out. She doesn't do gum."

Ash? I remembered hearing something about a new kid this week but hadn't paid attention beyond that.

Another girl whispered loud enough for everyone to hear, "*I'd* give you some if I had any."

A boy called out. "I'm sure he knows you'd give him way more than gum, Lexie." The class broke out in laughter.

Ms. Gable poked her head through the door. "That is quite enough! Get out your homework— and no conversing." She pulled the door shut again.

I bent to retrieve my homework from my bag, proud of the neatly printed equations that filled the page. That's when I saw them—my roll of spearmint breath mints. I wasn't sure what made me do it.

Maybe it was relief about feeling better. Maybe being sick had made me realize I was more like humans than I cared to admit. Whatever the reason, I popped one into my mouth and turned with the roll in my hand.

"I have a mint," I said, searching for the boy who'd spoken.

"Good God, she actually speaks," I heard from one corner of the room. Several girls snickered.

"You're an angel," said the voice.

I bit my tongue to keep from responding. *No, just a faery.* Technically, a half-faery, not that it mattered. We were hated by humans every bit as much as our full-fledged relatives. After everything that had happened during the Faery Wars, it was surprising that Disney still made movies that depicted faeries as cute and mischievous. Of course, there had been plenty of angry parents protesting outside the theaters with signs saying that Disney was "normalizing evil."

I twisted my head farther and spotted him in the last row, four seats behind me and over a row. He glanced toward the door then crept through the aisle until he reached my side, kneeling at my desk. I looked over into the greenest eyes I'd ever seen. His dark hair flopped down just shy of his eyes as he peered into mine. How had I not noticed him before? My ability to speak evaporated, and the fact that his hand was outstretched to accept the mint escaped me.

A slow grin spread across his face. My wings pushed against their restraints, trying to flutter. It took the sound of the classroom door opening for me to regain my senses.

"Sorry—here," I muttered, and dropped several mints into his hand.

"Thanks. I'm Ash, by the way." He turned to rush back to his seat.

"Well, Mr. Cooper, are you introducing yourself to each person individually, or is Lila Kincade just one lucky girl?" asked Ms. Gable.

"No, sorry, Ms. Gable," he responded.

The heat in my cheeks intensified and spread all the way down to my neck. *Pay no attention to the tomato-colored girl in front of you.*

"Good. Well then, let's begin," said Ms. Gable. "Who would like to take us through the first equation?"

I attempted—and failed—to distract myself with the numbers Ms. Gable wrote on the board. Although I faced the front of the room like the good student I was, Ash's green eyes flashed more than once through my mind. I was pretty sure that made me pathetic.

Of one thing I was very sure. In my entire life, my wings had never reacted the way they had when Ash looked at me.

I was in trouble.

ALSO BY KRISTI HELVIG

Wingless (Short Story Prequel)

The Wing Collector

The Burn Out Series

Burn Out

Strange Skies

Short Stories

Countdown Cafe *(TICK TOCK Anthology)*

The Boy Who Wasn't There *(OFF BEAT Anthology)*

The Missing *(DEAD NIGHT Anthology)*

ABOUT KRISTI HELVIG

Kristi Helvig is a Ph.D. Clinical Psychologist turned sci-fi/fantasy writer. You can find her musing about space monkeys, Star Trek, and other random topics on her blog. Kristi resides in sunny Colorado with her hubby, kids, and behaviorally-challenged dogs. Find out more about Kristi at www.kristihelvig.com.

MY FINAL GIFT

SUE DUFF

IT WAS THE DAY AFTER RUSSELL R. RATCHET'S fourteenth birthday when he saw a ghost.

He rolled onto his back and rubbed his sleep-crusted eyes, then stared at the paint-flaked ceiling. The stillness in the house licked chills along his spine. Where was Nana's racking cough? He pulled back the crocheted blanket and shivered at the bite in dawn's air. With a sharp inhale, he set his bare feet on the chipped linoleum and half-hobbled to the stairs but paused with his hand on the bannister. The quiet from upstairs magnified the beating of his heart and he walked up the creaking steps, instinct telling him no need to hurry.

The closer he drew to her bedroom, the familiar stink of moth balls grew heavy, and blended with mold and mildew wafting into the hall from the bathroom. The old farm house had seen its best days long before Russell came to live with his grandparents as a fretful three-year old.

Nana lay on her side with her back to the door, her frayed comforter pulled over her shoulder. Russell stepped around the bed and gazed at the only person who ever loved him more than life itself. His jaw clenched, and he reached out to brush away a strand of her blue hair that she swore was a natural gray, although he'd find a bottle of her home dye-jobs in the trash every few months.

His finger touched an ice cube. With a whimper, he knelt beside the bed as tears welled in his lower lids. "Nana," he whispered, giving her shoulder a gentle shake. He held his breath to push back the sob.

When the time comes, she had rasped a couple nights ago, *get Burt. He'll know what to do.*

Russell got to his feet and swiped his face across his pajama sleeve. He donned his dingy coveralls and cracked-soled boots, biked the five miles and woke up the town's handyman who answered the door in his bathrobe and jeans. He apparently didn't keep farmer hours like the rest of the county's citizens.

"My Nana," Russell announced in a soft voice. "I think she's dead."

Burt's eyes widened. "Why didn't you call?" He stuck his head out and looked around. "You shouldn't have risked coming here."

Russell hesitated at the handyman's reaction "The phone got shut off last week."

"Throw your bike in the back of my truck." Burt hesitated. "Lock yourself inside the cab. Don't open it for anyone but me."

Russell hefted the heavy bike over the side of the pickup. It slid and scraped across the bed. On a typical day, his nerves would have quivered from the noise, but not today. A strange numbness had set in, a shield keeping everything around him at bay.

He let himself inside Burt's cab, locked the doors as instructed, and waited. He studied the surrounding landscape. The handyman lived on the outskirts of town, but small homes were scattered farther down the dirt road. Russell wasn't sure what, or who he should be looking out for while he scanned the horizon.

A handful of minutes later, Burt unlocked the driver's door, and it opened with a creak. He slid his shotgun behind the seats and got in. The handy man's snowy hair was greased back in combed ruts across his scalp and his dark shirt smelled of detergent.

Burt started the truck and shifted into gear. Russell focused on the road leading out of town while his bike rattled in the truck bed behind them. The numb sensation gave into brooding questions. "Why'd you bring a gun?" he asked.

The handyman's jaw bulged, and he looked out the back window. "There's things your Nana should've told you Russell. Me and her got in nasty pissing matches about it." He glanced in the rearview mirror every couple of seconds or so. "Your father's bound to come for you, now that your Nana can't protect you anymore."

"She told me he was dead," Russell said.

"Wanting it to be true doesn't make it so," Burt muttered.

"If my father's alive, does that mean I don't have to go into foster care?" His eighth-grade teacher, Mrs. Kroeger, had shown him brochures she'd picked up from social services. *You'll have a family, Russell,* she said during last month's meeting. *Brothers and sisters to hang out with and to play games with.* He didn't want to live in a strange house with strange folk. But everyone, including Nana, said he couldn't stay and work the farm by himself. The word *foreclosure* had seeped into Russell's nightmares long before he understood what it meant.

"First, I gotta see what's going on at the house, then I'll know what to do with you," Burt said.

Russell's questions gained momentum as the truck sped down the dirt road. Nana claimed he had no other family. Why had she lied about his father?

WITH THE SHOTGUN braced under his arm, Burt rested his hand on the finial at the base of the staircase. He gazed up the stairs, then cocked his ear for a few seconds. The handyman felt Russell's coveralls and rustled his hair. "Did you wash up before you fetched me?"

"No sir," Russell said. "I put on clothes and biked to your place."

"Better stay down here," Burt said. He ascended slow and steady with the gun pointed ahead of him.

Other than Nana's body, what was he expecting? Russell pushed against the wall, every muscle tense and at the ready. When no cries of alarm or gunshots rang out, Russell entered the kitchen and stared at the dirty dishes from his birthday dinner which Nana had been too tired to eat. Flies feasted on the untouched cupcake he'd biked into town to buy for his celebration. One of Nana's coughing fits blew out his candle the second she'd lit it. If you didn't make a wish for your birthday, could it bring bad luck? Was he somehow responsible for her demise?

"You need to pack your things. Time to go," Burt announced from the doorway. He set the shotgun on the kitchen table. "How are you holding up?"

Russell swiped at his damp cheeks and faced Burt. "Nana said you'd know what to do. What did she mean?"

"She entrusted me to get you out of here and take you to a safe place," Burt said. "Somewhere your father can't find you."

Russell's biological father had run off when Russell was a toddler. His mom had never talked about him. Nana said he'd drunk himself to death years ago. If his father was still alive, wouldn't he have to go with him? He eyed the shotgun. "Why do you need that? What has you so spooked?"

"Your father's a twisted soul, Russell." Burt put a gentle hand on his shoulder. "Grab what you can carry and any money you have. We need to get out of here."

"I don't think there's any money left." Russell regretted the lie. The loose change in his pocket felt cool against his thigh. A sizeable shadow snuck into the kitchen and obscured the sun's warmth. A shiver struck Russell, and he grabbed his arms.

Burt snatched the shotgun off the table. "Keep your head down and lock the doors behind me!"

Russell jumped as a spurt of adrenaline raced through him. He grabbed a knife from the kitchen drawer.

The handyman exited through the front, letting the screen door bang shut behind him. He paused several feet from the house, then turned in all directions with the shotgun held at the ready.

Russell followed him to the front of the house. He ducked low and peered over the edge of the front window. Other than Burt, nothing moved. A heartbeat later, sunlight reflected off something farther down the road.

Burt called out over his shoulder. "I'll be back. Don't open the door for anyone!" He grabbed his keys from his pocket and jumped in his truck. The tip of the shotgun stuck out the driver's window.

The truck backed up, then jerked to a stop. Burt got out, grabbed Russell's bike and set it on the ground without bothering to set the kickstand.

When it landed, a thin cloud of dust rose around it. Burt drove off.

Russell ran around the house, checking and double checking the latches on the windows and doors. Then he returned to Nana's room and peered out her front window. Burt's truck had left a slight trail of dust, but as Russell stared through the brown veil, he lost sight of the vehicle and couldn't tell if it ended up in a ditch or had disappeared over the crest of the hill.

His stomach lurched and twisted into a knot, and droplets of perspiration dripped down his chest despite the chill in the room. He pressed a fist to his abdomen and turned away from the window. Burt had covered Nana's face with the sheet. Russell pulled it back as far as her chin and stood at the foot of her bed for what seemed like forever while the weight of his future bent his back. A pounding at his temples soon turned deafening. He pushed fists against his ears to stop the surging headache from tearing his skull apart. Russell dropped to one knee and grabbed her footboard.

A minute later, the pounding transformed into a tortuous drone, and he slumped onto the floor. His thoughts drifted as the room morphed into ebony shadows that swallowed everything around him.

RUSSELL BLINKED BACK TO CONSCIOUSNESS. The headache had passed. He rose on shaky legs, startled that he was in the bathroom down the hall from Nana's room. A damp towel lay beside him.

At a creak from the direction of the stairs, Russell called out. "Burt?"

No answer.

He quietly made his way to the bannister and peered over the edge. The rooms below offered familiar shadows, but no sounds other than the tick tock of Nana's grandfather clock in the front room.

He needed to pack, but what about money? They didn't have fifty bucks, much less anything else of real value that he could pawn. They'd slaughtered the sole remaining cow several months ago. *It'll sustain us till your birthday,* Nana said. Russell had often wondered about the curious goal she set for the final months of her life; she was determined to stay alive to celebrate his fourteenth birthday.

Russell packed his knapsack but paused at his mother's picture sitting on the dresser. When he was five, her death was declared a hit and run by the Macon County Coroner, although some parts of her body were never found. He removed it from the frame and stuffed it in the outer pocket of his sack. Russell did the same with the picture of Nana and Papa. His grandfather's end came at the hands of a rickety platform and a nineteen-fifties thresher with no safety switch. No one bothered to sort his parts. At least Nana had a natural death, if you counted lung cancer as natural.

Russell checked downstairs, then studied the surrounding area beyond the front stoop. All was calm. He grabbed the cleaver off the kitchen hook and gathered the nerve to venture outside. It struck him that he wouldn't know his father if he walked up. There'd never been any pictures of him among his family's things. Not even at Nana and Papa's house.

Your father's a twisted soul. Russell shuddered.

Papa kept an old tin of money for emergencies. Russell had seen him stash it in the barn. He peered out the front window and found the driveway empty. Whatever had Burt spooked, the handyman was either still chasing it, or leading it away from Russell. He unlocked the kitchen door and ran to the barn, then rummaged around, looking for the stash of money. The tin was in a tool drawer, but all he discovered was a faded IOU from a neighbor who'd passed away from complications of gout a couple years earlier.

A shadow danced beyond the slats outside the barn. Russell gripped the cleaver tight and raised it above his head, but the shadow failed to reappear. He hadn't heard Burt's truck. "Who's there?"

The lack of response didn't ease the throbbing pulse at Russell's neck.

"You need to get out of here."

Russell dropped the cleaver and fell backwards with a yelp, landing hard on his rear. Nana was on a bale of hay. His hands slipped on the straw-littered ground while scooting away from the talking dead. "What the hell!"

"You can't stay, Russell. You need to get on your bike and take off," she said.

It was like looking at Nana through a grimy glass. She appeared to hover above the bale and her skin was the color of putty with blotches of gray.

"Russell R. Ratchet, you need to high tail it out of here." She pointed toward the dented red can sitting at the base of the tractor. "First, take care of the house."

"But Burt—."

Her voice fell along with her eyes. "Your father killed him. It's up to you to save yourself."

"I don't even know him!" Russell yelled. "What does he want with me?"

Nana's ghostly eyes grew dark. "He's after your soul, Russell."

She didn't make any sense. "Why are you a ghost? How can you talk? Why do I see you?" The questions poured out of him like a gushing faucet.

"Stay focused," Nana urged. "Burn the house down. It'll buy you some time to get away."

"Why'd you lie to me?" he shouted, but Nana disappeared without responding. He scrambled to his feet. What diesel was left inside the fuel can sloshed about at his knee as he lugged it back to the house.

He needed answers, but whenever Nana returned, she'd disappear the second he paused to ask. He'd never won an argument with the old woman and now that she was a ghost, he had less of a chance.

He did his best to hold his breath while sprinkling the diesel about. He left the empty can in the kitchen. The only thing missing was the match. Nana had left them on the counter after lighting his birthday candle.

Russell stepped outside, then paused, regarding the crooked structure. His fingers trembled. He couldn't bring himself to strike the match. "I can't do this to you, even if you are dead."

Nana put a hand on Russell's shoulder. It went numb and tingled at the same time as if freezing and thawing could be simultaneous. "Cremation doesn't cost anything but a strong will."

IT DIDN'T TAKE LONG for the blaze to consume the house. Once Russell reached the top of the hill, he paused to catch his breath. He watched the smoke rise to the heavens and imagined Nana lifted on its darkening pillow.

"Keep moving," Nana said.

"No." Russell reached toward her but stopped short of connecting with her ghostly image. "Not till you tell me why you're so scared of my father."

"Haven't you sensed the chill in the air, the moving shadows where there shouldn't be any? He's got powers beyond this world." Her attention fell to the flames below and her voice grew tense. "He's here."

The flames had changed color and were now purple. At the center of the blaze, they danced to a rhythm in contrast to the rest. The blaze had grown to twice the width of the house. A spark shot toward the stacked hay bales between the house and the barn, and they, too, burst into flames. The barn would be next.

"Get out of here!" Nana screamed.

Thick smoke blew in his direction. He took off, focused on outrunning the blaze.

RUSSELL HAD PEDALED ten or more miles before he dared to rest. His chest ached, and he fought to take a breath. When he slipped off his bike, his legs turned to mush, and he slumped to the ground, not caring that his bike tipped over and fell.

The second Russell regained his strength, he sat up to take heed of the billowing cloud of various grays at the horizon. A swirling mass, much like a dust devil, emerged from its center. As he watched, it broke free like it had a mind of its own.

It was no longer part of the wildfire smoke, but something unworldly. Goose bumps popped out along his arms.

Nana appeared between him and the approaching gray dust devil. "Head for the gulley!"

Russell took off, running with everything he had.

He closed the twenty yards in a matter of seconds and slid into the crevice feet first. He landed on the hard dirt floor, then scrambled on all fours toward a cluster of boulders, deposited by years of flash floods. The knapsack was too bulky, and he threw it off to the side, so he could wedge himself out of sight between the rocks. He hunkered down, pulling his tan jacket over his head.

He didn't have long to wait. The thunderous wind dipped into the gulley like a freight train on a designated track and headed toward him. The swirling wind swept over the boulders where Russell hid, kicking up debris and making it harder to breathe. A frigid chill penetrated Russell's bones, and he trembled. Wails of what sounded like a hundred tortured souls pierced his ears.

The swirling wind moved farther down the gulley. By the sound of it, they either dispersed or found a new track across the plain.

Dust coated Russell's nose and throat. He stifled coughs the best he could, but remained crouched, unwilling to give his position away.

"It might return," Nana said. "Head for the interstate."

"What's going on?" When she didn't respond, he peered above the boulders and discovered he was alone. The surrounding calm gave him courage to emerge. Nana's ghost was gone along with his knapsack.

Russell climbed out of the gulley, swiping at his grimy clothes, and retrieved his bike. It was caked in dust, but otherwise intact. From the intermittent glow of lights at the horizon, the interstate was at least a couple miles away, an eternity given his sore muscles. He fought the fatigue and biked toward the highway but glanced over his shoulder every few yards. It didn't help that he was parched, and his stomach raged war, screaming to be fed.

When he arrived at the edge of the road, there was plenty of interstate traffic that came and went every few minutes. Truckers, families in cars, businessmen, making their way to the sprawling cities to scrape out a living. Passersby on a mission, not bothering to stop and pick up a scrawny, filthy teen with an old bike.

Nana hovered nearby but remained mute, refusing to answer his questions. Every muscle in Russell's body ached and the empty pit in his stomach ceased to rumble. A couple hours later a white pickup slowed, then swerved onto the side of the road. An arm stuck out the driver's side and waved when Russell didn't react. "Come on, get in," the man shouted out the window.

Nana floated ahead and peered inside the truck. She gestured for him to come. He grabbed his bike and approached with cautious steps. The dusty pickup was a newer model. When he stuck his face in the passenger window, he caught a whiff of cologne mixed with river water. The older, plump driver wore dark waders supported by wide suspenders. A bamboo fly rod reached from the foot of the passenger side, between the bucket seats and out the back-sliding window.

The man's jovial face was the most inviting thing Russell had seen in a while. "Thank you." Russell loaded his bike in the truck bed, then let himself in the passenger seat, careful not to bend the fly rod. Nana sat on his lap and Russell did his best not to acknowledge her. He gave the man a grateful nod.

"My name's Doc Harvey," the driver said.

"Russell." He eyed the partially drained water bottle in the cup holder.

Doc Harvey studied him for a moment. "How old are you?"

"Sixteen," Russell lied. He was already a foot taller than most of the boys in his class and hair had sprouted on his upper lip a couple months earlier.

If the man questioned Russell's age, his expression didn't show it. "Where you headed?"

"Anywhere my father won't find me."

"No other family?"

"No sir. My Nana died, and I'm alone. I really need your help." Russell cleared his throat from behind his fist. "If you can get me to a town where I can find work, I'd be much obliged. I'm a hard worker and can earn my way."

Doc Harvey reached into a cooler behind the seat and handed Russell a bottle of water. He unscrewed it and gulped half of it down before stopping.

"I've got some granola bars in the glove compartment. Help yourself." Doc Harvey pulled out onto the interstate and the truck picked up speed. "You swear you got no other family, boy?"

"Other than my good for nothing father," Russell said. "There's no one."

Doc Harvey glanced at Russell out of the corner of his eye. "Then I know just the place."

PART TWO

NIOBRARA COUNTY, WYOMING, 2007

RUSSELL WHEELED HIS CUSTODIAN'S CART OFF TO ONE side. He stared at the body bag on the gurney as Kurt pushed it toward him and he wondered if this one would hold any treasures. It'd been a while since a murder or interesting corpse had passed through Doc Harvey's small county morgue at the border of Wyoming and Nebraska. Lately it had been old ranchers having heart attacks and drunk teenager accidents. What Russell had come to think of as the backcountry plague of the young.

A ghost poked his head out of Russell's cart. "Who's that?" the old rancher asked.

"Don't know, don't care," Russell muttered. The guy had been killed in a truck accident a couple weeks ago. "Why are you still here?"

"I don't have anywhere else to be," the rancher said.

"You're nothing but a pest!" Russell hissed. Kurt looked up from the gurney and gave him a skeptical glance. Russell swiped at the ghost like he was swooshing flies. "Just be gone, already," he mumbled under his breath.

The old rancher's ghost disappeared.

"What's for sale, Russell Stover?" Kurt quipped as he wheeled the body past Russell.

"A box of chocolates," Russell said in the retort that had grown stale after eighteen months. He'd never mustered the courage to add, *filled with nuts like you.*

Instead of his typical comeback, though, Kurt grabbed Russell by the back of the neck and pressed his face toward the body bag.

"Care to take a look?" Kurt unzipped the bag far enough for Russell to hover over the corpse's face. A pale, bearded man's face stared up at him. No one had bothered to lower the man's eyelids. "Maybe all you need is a whiff." The morgue assistant let go of Russell's neck, and with a deep growl, he wheeled the gurney toward the swinging double doors.

Russell was tempted to stick his mop in the gurney's path and send Kurt face down onto the corpse. But his need to retaliate was overshadowed by the likelihood Kurt would beat him to within an inch of his life later, during his break.

He stared at the morgue assistant. Their routine exchanges were as mundane as their surroundings. Why was Kurt so aggressive today?

"What'd I do to piss you off?" Russell asked.

"I'm tired of babysitting your sorry ass," Kurt said without turning around. The morgue assistant pressed the blue handicapped button on the wall with his elbow and the doors swung open. He and the gurney disappeared around the corner and the doors closed on his shadow.

"I don't need a babysitter," Russell muttered. Not for the first time, he wondered why the entrance to the afterlife needed handicapped access. He stuck his mop in the bucket and sloshed sudsy water across the floor. The linoleum was clean and unmarred, so different from the floor in Nana's house. It was Russell's job to make sure it stayed that way. No small feat considering the surrounding roads were more dirt than asphalt, and Doc Harvey, who doubled as the county coroner and local undertaker, had a passion for daily fly fishing. He often arrived at the morgue day or night, dragging in weeds and river muck, still wearing his waders with bamboo rod in hand.

Russell's stomach lurched and rumbled. A deep throbbing headache formed. The unpleasant sensations were appearing more frequent, but never morphed into something severe enough to mention to Doc Harvey.

He turned up the sound on his thrift store iPod and went about his custodial duties welcoming the ensuing trance that always took the symptoms away. He swung his hips to a favorite song and mopped his way toward the abyss at the end of the hall.

"Russell?" Evie, the morgue receptionist-slash-secretary called out from the front office. "Russell!"

He blinked. He was hunched over the sink in the janitor's closet. His face was damp, and drips from his hair wet his cheeks. He raked his fingers through his hair and stuck his head out the doorway. "What?" he asked.

Evie removed the clip at the back of her head and her ebony hair fell across one side of her olive complexion face. She was pushing fifty, but still had a youthful attitude reflected by her mini-skirts and fake nails. "Have you seen Dusty? I put food in his bowl this morning, but it's still there. He always eats by now."

Russell shook his head and it helped to clear his thoughts. "No, I haven't seen him."

"Make sure he eats before you leave. Give him a treat from my bottom drawer." She adjusted the strap of her purse higher on her shoulder and blew him a kiss.

The place quieted as Evie and the still-disgruntled Kurt buzzed out the front doors and into their vehicles like bees returning to their separate hives. Russell locked the front door.

This was his favorite time of day, when his co-workers didn't interrupt the music blaring through his earbuds, and sunlight faded into artful shadows that changed throughout the night by the glow of a migrating moon. This evening, it hovered at the horizon, as bright and round as a dinner plate. Its glow lit the hallways in varying shades of gray that reminded him of Nana's hair.

Russell finished emptying the trash and vacuuming the front office. He didn't feel like playing video games in his room upstairs, so he checked the contents of the breakroom refrigerator. Every week, Evie and Doc placed containers of leftovers inside with his name on them. He grabbed the brown paper sack and peered inside. It looked like one of Doc's roast beef sandwiches, chips and an apple. He set the lunch on top of his empty trash bag for later.

He wheeled his cart through the double doors, pressing the blue button with the reverence that it deserved. He entered the autopsy room, the back sanctum of the building, what had proven to be a lifeline to his sanity. He enjoyed being among the guests of the morgue.

He'd lost his revulsion of corpses that fateful day while standing in Nana's bedroom. He preferred the dead over most of the living he'd encountered since outrunning the supernatural flames and odd dust devil that hadn't reappeared since. Skittish and paranoid, he'd kept mostly to the morgue, rarely venturing beyond the main street outside.

Doc Harvey, Evie and Kurt had become his family. Sheriff Nighthorse, too, although Russell had been on edge around the sheriff at first. But he seemed to take Russell at his word and as far as he knew, the sheriff had never verified where Russell came from. Doc gave him a job, and he, Kurt and Russell cleared out the morgue attic. Evie transformed it into a comfy bedroom, making the curtains herself.

The chilled air in the examination room set Russell's teeth chattering.

"You're nothing but skin and bones."

He turned to find Nana floating near the wall. "Where have you been?" he asked. It'd been a few weeks since she'd made an appearance.

"I got bored," she said. "But unlike you, I don't live here."

"Ghosts take a vacation?" he asked.

"You could, too, if you didn't spend what little you make on zombie video games," she said.

Russell shrugged. "I like killing things that don't fight back."

"I'd kick your sorry ass out of your bean bag if I was still alive," Nana said. She floated past Russell and put a translucent hand on the body bag Kurt had wheeled in earlier. "This one's a keeper."

Kurt had slid the bag onto the metal table that Russell polished to a mirror shine in between autopsies. Doc Harvey must be expected, otherwise Kurt would have put the body in the freezer. The dim light offered enough muted glow for Russell to discover the zipper had been pulled down and the bag left open.

It took but a glance for Russell to tell that the guy had lived an exciting life. Tattoos covered his chest and arms with their stories of past girlfriends and a declaration of love for his mother.

She leaned in, focused on the flame tattoo on the man's shoulder. "Ever been tempted to get one?" she asked.

"Nope," he said without hesitation.

Nana chuckled. "You screamed every time I pulled out a needle to remove your splinters."

"Sticking the needle in a flame to get it red hot might have had something to do with it." Russell grabbed the chart at the same time he withdrew the rag sticking out from his back pocket. He wiped the table around the bag as Nana read the police report.

"Drago Smith," she said.

"Explains the enormous dragon tattoo." He swiped at a red smudge on the floor. Whatever it was had spread to the toe of his boot.

"Member of the Hells Angels. Gunned down in a barroom brawl around four this morning," she continued. "Out on Route 151."

Russell paused. The body should have been picked up by Cheyenne. Why bring it two counties away? He noticed that the dragon tattoo had a wide staring eye above the man's left pec. Upon closer inspection, it was a small caliber bullet hole. Someone either had precise aim or got off a lucky shot. Russell took a moment to imagine the man's final seconds of life; smashing a chair over someone's head, landing a concussive punch to another man's jaw. In between, taking a swig of a beer or kissing the waitress. He bent over the body and took a strong whiff. The man smelled of urine and cheap cigarettes.

"God, I miss my Marlboros," she said.

"He pissed himself." Russell turned away from the corpse.

"Tell me something I don't know." She waved her hand in front of her face.

"You can't smell," he countered.

"Memory is stronger than anyone gives it credit for," she said. "Ever heard of a phantom limb? I got a friend that still carries on about his missing leg. Been two-hundred years but he gets the sniffles just thinking about it. He yaps on and on about it."

Russell remembered Dusty. "You haven't seen the dog today, have you?"

Nana's eyes widened at the same time her jovial demeanor vanished. "Is it missing?"

"No one's seen him all day." He stuck his head out into the hall. "Dusty!" he shouted. Silence. The dog often hung out with Russell after Evie left since allergies prevented her from taking him home. Russell tried to recall the last time he'd seen him and decided it was the previous night.

He turned away from the body and wiped down the empty gurney Kurt had positioned next to the wall. It was against regulations. The morgue assistant was supposed to wheel it out of the room and leave it in the hall because of cross-contamination or something like that. Russell never understood why they'd be worried a dead body would catch a cold or if it even could. He didn't care enough to ask and figured checking out the dead bodies after hours wouldn't be allowed either.

Russell's elbow connected with the body bag at the man's feet. The bulge collapsed under his weight. He pressed down on the lower section of the bag. The man's body ended at the hip. He grabbed the clipboard and squinted in the dull light, struggling to make out Kurt's scribble. It didn't say anything about the biker missing the lower half of his body. He unzipped the bag farther, and discovered torn flesh, and exposed bone.

Russell found himself obsessing over the corpse in the morgue. He hoped the biker's ghost would make an appearance and he returned to the autopsy room every half hour to check.

At two o'clock in the morning he sat down in the hall outside the autopsy room and pulled his untouched lunch from the bag. He nibbled on the sandwich, contemplating how a man could lose half his body in a gunfight. Why was such a crucial bit of information missing in the report? He racked his memory trying to recall if the body was intact when Kurt rolled it past him, but he had been focused on the morgue assistant's irritation and not the bag.

"I'm too old to sit on the floor." Nana groaned as she settled beside him. Given that she didn't have any rickety bones or rusty joints to speak of, Russell decided it was that memory thing she mentioned earlier. "Be honest with me, boy. Did you eat him?"

"What?" He choked on the bit of roast beef and dry bread.

"The biker. Were you hungry?" She stared at him with the same intensity that used to give him shivers.

"Does it look like I'm starving?" He held up his half-eaten sandwich.

"Someone did." She turned a keen eye toward him.

"Don't you mean some*thing*?" But her question piqued his curiosity. He got to his feet, entered the autopsy room and felt along the bag where the man's lower half should have been.

"Cowboy up, boy," Nana mumbled.

"You never did have any patience."

"You're stalling. Get on with it," she said.

He drew a sharp inhale, unzipped the bag to what should have been the man's knees and grabbed the small flashlight from his belt. The beam of light lit up the corpse. Nana was right. The ripped and torn tissue reminded Russell of one of their cows that had been attacked. Nana claimed a coyote had done it.

She hovered across from Russell. "Something, or someone, ate him." Russell caught a note of real concern in her voice. "If the biker had all his parts when he was put into the ambulance, but not when he was brought here . . ." Nana floated away like something weighed on her mind.

He checked the large-faced clock on the wall. It was well after two in the morning. "Where is Doc Harvey?" he asked.

"Maybe the bully forgot to let him know a body came in," Nana said.

"I need to get to bed, but I can't just leave the

body sitting out if Doc's not coming," Russell said. A sound came from the double doors at the end of the hallway. "Dusty?" he called out.

The mutt had to be wandering about. It was the dead of night. Doc would have entered from the back door. No one else would have a reason to be here, especially in the front office area. Russell never thought of the morgue-mortuary as creepy, but unease set his senses on high alert. He entered the hall and pushed open the double doors at the far end. Russell whistled. "Dusty, come here boy."

Silence hovered in the air. "Kurt?" Had the morgue assistant realized he never connected with Doc and decided to return in the middle of the night to take care of the body?

When the sound didn't repeat itself, Russell returned and focused on the body at hand. It was up to him to make this right. Put the body on ice, then head upstairs.

Shuffling scrapes across linoleum triggered goose bumps along Russell's arms. It came from beyond the swinging double doors at the end of the hall.

"Kurt?" The morgue assistant must be teasing Russell. "Okay Kurt, stop with the fun and games. I know it's you," he shouted. When Kurt didn't answer,

Russell closed the autopsy room door, but the fan circulating the cold air drowned out everything and made him feel more vulnerable.

He cracked open the door and listened with everything he had. The padding scrapes could be Dusty's. But it occurred to Russell that if an animal had made the biker a meal, it could still be inside the building.

Light leapt into the far end of the hall as the double doors parted. A whip-like shadow stretched along the wall, across from Russell's hiding spot inside the autopsy room. The image danced back and forth like a snake mesmerized by a flute player's tune. The whip was replaced by a looming dark form on the hallway wall. With each padding, scratching scrape, the figure grew until it flooded the wall with impending doom.

"Who's there?" a familiar voice called out.

Russell straightened his back and exhaled, unaware he'd been holding his breath. "Doc?"

The door swung into the autopsy room. Doc Harvey reached inside and felt along the wall for the light switch. A second later, dim light filled the space. It grew brighter as Doc turned the round dial. The country doctor stood in his waders with a fishing rod in hand.

"What are you doing here?" Doc asked. "Why are you standing in the dark?"

"I wasn't sure if I needed to move the body into the cooler before I left," Russell said.

Doc entered and set his fishing rod on the empty gurney. "Don't try a stunt like that, not alone. You could throw your scrawny back out."

"Yes sir." Russell grabbed the box of latex gloves sitting nearby and followed Doc Harvey to the sink. He scrubbed his hands and forearms with the powdered soap from the dispenser and grabbed the paper towel from the pile. He pushed his enormous fingers into the nearby gloves and snapped them tight around his wrists.

"You can go to bed, Russell. No need for you to remain."

"I'm not tired, sir." Russell tossed him a pleading, tight-lipped smile. "Can I stay?"

"If you're going to assist me, we better make it official." Doc picked up a scalpel and adopted a stoic expression. "In honor of your months of dedicated service to this morgue and coroner's office, I hereby appoint you temporary morgue assistant." He touched each of Russell's shoulders with the flat side of the blade.

Russell lowered his head. "I am honored to serve,

your majesty." He chuckled at a rubbery whiff of Doc's waders.

Doc spread apart the unzipped bag. If he was shocked at the missing lower half, the old man masked it well. He grabbed the clipboard and ran his latex finger down the page. A string of expletives passed the old doctor's lips. "Bikers can't keep their guns in their pockets." He touched the dragon's eye and stuck the tip of his pinky finger into the hole.

Russell's stomach lurched, and acid burned his throat as his roast beef threatened a return visit. He took shallow, quick breaths through his nose to still the ensuing gag.

Doc gave him a quizzical stare. "You okay, boy?"

"Yes, sir." Russell suppressed the nausea and focused on the body.

Doc looked at the clipboard without pulling his finger out of the wound. "I can't feel the bullet. Help me turn him onto his side." Russell positioned himself across the table. "Better put gloves on."

Russell inhaled the powdery latex smell and stretched them onto his hands. It was a shot of adrenaline like no other as he imagined himself a surgeon about to open a living, breathing, heart-pumping patient to reveal the intricate workings of the human body. Doc grabbed the man's shoulders while Russell took over at the man's hips, and they rolled him onto his side.

Doc felt around the man's back and leaned in close. "It didn't exit," he muttered more to himself than to Russell. "Hard to believe he lasted long enough to be killed by a motorcycle accident."

"Why do you think that?" Russell asked.

"The fact he got cut in two. Sometimes the force of the collision is so great, the upper body keeps moving when the lower half is pinned to the bike. It rips the body apart." Doc gazed at the sizable wound beneath the biker's hips, pinching and then pushing aside tendons. He leaned closer, running his finger over the jagged bone.

"I thought something ate him," Russell said as they rolled him onto his back.

Doc Harvey stared at Russell. He grabbed the chart and flipped the single sheet over. "It says the man had been in a gunfight, but there's nothing in the highway patrol's notes about it ending in a motorcycle accident." The old doctor set the chart on the edge of the table and grabbed his headband from the cabinet drawer. He adjusted it around his head and switched on the light. It looked out of place with the Doc's waders. He removed other instruments from plastic wrappers. "Did Kurt say anything when he brought him in?" Doc bent over and examined the lower wound.

"No," Russell said. "He just wheeled it in like always." Stomach acid fought its way to the surface, but he kept it from bringing anything with it.

"This is definitely not a cut of any kind," Doc said.

"How can you tell?" Russell asked.

"The edge of the bones leading to both missing legs are scraped, like they were gnawed." Doc's bushy eyebrows clamped together, like his brain was working overtime.

"So, an animal did it." Russell's nerves revved along with the pulse in his veins.

"There's no animal large enough in these parts that could do something like that." Doc zipped up the body bag. "We get trampled bodies and steer horns that have penetrated torsos. Nothing like this." He stared at Russell. "Do you remember anything from earlier? After Kurt wheeled the body in?"

"I was cleaning." But that wasn't entirely true. He'd had one of his blackouts.

"Told you." Nana appeared beside Russell. She gave Doc a smug expression despite his inability to see her. Russell did his best to ignore her.

"Have you seen the biker's ghost yet?" Nana asked. Russell gave her a subtle shake of his head.

"You need to tell the boy the truth," Doc Harvey said. "Otherwise, I will."

Russell froze. Doc was looking at Nana. The corner of her mouth drew up in a snarl, the exposed teeth were brighter than the rest.

"Who are you talking to?" Russell whispered.

"Me," Nana hissed.

Doc grabbed the handle on a cooler door and opened it. "I need to get a hold of the others," he announced.

"You can see her?" Russell's tone was tinged in anger.

Doc paused. "I know you have questions, Russell. I will do my best to answer them. But first, we need to put this poor soul in the cooler."

Grudgingly, Russell complied, and they hefted the corpse onto the sliding tray. It slid inside with little effort. Doc shut the door and made sure the latch was secure.

Russell turned on Nana. "How can he see you? But she crossed her arms and raised her chin. The same response he always got whenever she refused to give him the answers he craved. He'd stopped wasting his breath months ago. But no more.

Her chest lifted and then fell with an imagined sigh. "Paranormal beings can see ghosts, Russell. Doc has seen me since he picked us up that night."

"It's what told me you were one of us," Doc said. "And why I gave you a home here." Doc dropped the gloves in the trash and grabbed his rod off the gurney.

"What do you mean, you're paranormal?" Russell asked.

"I'm a Lycan."

"You're a werewolf?" Russell backed away from the country doctor. "I don't understand," he stammered.

"You're a Death Eater, Russell." Nana threw Doc a dark look. "We come from a long line of them. Your great-grandfather was one, I was . . . you."

"My father?" Russell asked. Her gaze lowered in response. "What's a Death Eater?" He looked at his hands, turning them over, looking for any sign out of the ordinary. He was a normal teenager, he silently insisted. "I'm not a monster."

"Your Death Eater emerges at the smell of death," she said. "But not always. You've resisted your true nature and we've encouraged it. I didn't want you to turn into a monster like your father. But he recently picked up your trail."

"Since then, we've done our best to get you food, so you'd be ready, in case he found you," Doc said.

It dawned on Russell that Doc wasn't referring to the leftovers in the kitchen. Acid burned his throat and he tried to swallow, but the half-eaten sandwich wouldn't stay down. Russell rushed over and threw up in the trash can. There was something odd about the chunks mixed with stomach acid. The phlegm was dark and had slivers of what looked like bone. At the sight, he emptied his stomach, the undeniable evidence piling up, then he turned away and washed his face in the sink.

When his senses cleared, he dried his face with the paper towels Doc handed him. "Getting me food. Like transporting a body from two counties away?" *I'm tired of babysitting you*, Kurt's words rang in Russell's ears. The morgue assistant's growing irritability, his making sure Russell got a whiff of Drago's corpse on the way in. The increasing blackouts. "Kurt knows?"

"He's a Lycan, like me," Doc said with a tinge of pride. "Evie's a gypsy."

"Does Sheriff Nighthorse know about us?" he asked.

Doc gave him a reassuring nod. "He's a shape shifter."

Russell wrapped his arms around his waist and sucked air to keep the dry heaves at bay. "Feeding me . . . to get ready for what?"

"To face your father and his army of trapped souls." Nana floated across the room.

"Why would he be after me?"

Nana shook her head. "Your father has spent most of his life embracing the monster within him. He has lost his humanity.

"Death Eaters aren't supposed to kill, only scavenge," Doc said.

"Your father is killing humans, Russell. We fear he'll turn on the paranormal race, if he hasn't already."

"How is that any different than humans" Russell asked.

"Because if he feeds on them, he'll inherit their powers," Doc said.

"And be unstoppable."

The edge in Nana's voice scraped Russell's nerves. His father was a cold-blooded killer. And he had targeted Russell.

"Stay here," Doc said. "I'll be back with reinforcements." His exit left the room cold and foreboding.

Russell's legs threatened to give out and he

leaned against the wall. "I eat the dead."

"When you do, you create a ghost. Most of them stick to you like an ethereal limb, and you can command them."

Nana was often around, had been since the day she died. The truth slammed into Russell like a hurricane and he stumbled back. "I ate you?"

"After Burt left me. When the fool chose to chase down your father instead of sticking with you. If he'd only kept you downstairs."

Russell slumped to the floor. "Is that why you wanted me to burn down the house? So, no one would discover your mutilated body?"

"That, and to destroy anything your father could use to find you," she said.

Russell's stomach lurched at the acrid odor wafting out of the trash and his thoughts fell upon the missing dog. He hadn't emptied the garbage into the Dumpster this evening. He bolted to his feet and ran out the back door. He stood still and stared at the Dumpster in the alley. A horde of flies created a buzzing chorus. The rusty hinges creaked when he lifted the lid, and the smell nearly knocked him to his knees. The swarm engulfed Russell's head. He directed his swats at their sound unable to track their divebomb attacks in the moonlight.

Even in the poorly lit Dumpster, Russell recognized Dusty's golden coat of fur. His heart sank. It was mottled with dark patches. He climbed up, balancing the edge of his shoe on the lower lip of the Dumpster, and he touched Dusty with his free hand. The dark patch at the dog's throat was sticky. His clenched throat cut off his scream. Russell fell backwards. The lid slammed shut, and he landed on his rear in the middle of the alley. He coughed on the rising dust and scooted until his back pressed against the wall of the nearby building.

Nana appeared. "Get back inside!"

"Did I do that?" Russell swiped his bloodied hand on the ground but managed to cake it in mud, rather than ridding it of the blood. It took everything he had not to wipe it on his jeans.

"You're not a killer," Nana said.

A deep, resonant growl came at the far end of the alley. A shadow rose high on the opposite wall, starting with an elongated snout that morphed into a wolf-like head. The pointed ears pulled back, pressing against the skull and giving the shadow a distorted appearance. The snout tipped upward and a thunderous howl filled the alley. The large mass turned in Russell's direction. It obliterated what little light was left.

Russell jumped to his feet and took off for the mortuary's back door, but it had locked behind him. He ran around to the front stoop. Something crackled beneath his sneakers. The overhead light bulb had been smashed. Bits of glass was scattered on the concrete steps.

An ominous dark cloud towered above the two-story buildings a couple blocks away. Russell's heart pounded as he tugged on the key ring hooked to his belt loop. He fumbled with the handful of keys, half of which he had no idea what they opened. The front door's key was larger than the rest, but in the moonlight, he couldn't tell one from another. The throaty rumble of the beast grew louder, and as the animal drew closer to this end of the alley, it's plodding paws slapped against the gravel.

The first three keys Russell found wouldn't enter the deadbolt, but the fourth one slipped deep inside with a scrape. No matter how much pressure he exerted, the damn thing wouldn't turn in either direction. The beast's shadow disappeared from the wall of the nearby building as though the moonlight devoured it.

The last key slipped inside the lock and turned with a loud metallic click. In one swift move, Russell pushed inside and slammed the door behind him.

He reset the deadbolt and slid to the floor with his chest lifting and falling to the erratic beat of his heart. A trickle of sweat snaked it way down his temple, and he swiped his brow. Too late, Russell realized he'd used his bloodied hand.

"Russell?" a voice called from the rear of the building. At approaching footsteps, Russell slid beneath the reception counter and pushed back against the wall.

A second later, the dim light streaming from the front window illuminated the lower half of a body. "Where the hell are you?" It was Kurt.

"Here." Russell poked his head out.

Kurt grabbed him and dragged him to his feet. "You were supposed to stay put in the autopsy room."

"Dusty's dead," Russell said. "He's in the alley Dumpster." His knees threatened to give out. "I think I ate him."

Kurt shook his head. "You don't kill things, Russell." His voice grew terse. "But your father might have."

Russell couldn't help but stare at Kurt like he was seeing him through a different lens. "Was that beast outside . . . you?"

"Doc called. Told me to get my butt over here."

Kurt's eyes grew black and he growled, deep and throaty. Russell never noticed till that moment how animalistic it sounded. Always had. "Do as you're told and stay inside from now on. Evie put a spell on the building and the surrounding lawn. It's the only place your Father can't touch you. Everyone will meet us here. I'll let the others in the back door." He disappeared down the hall.

Russell wandered out of the reception area, but he froze when a shimmering image slipped out between the double doors behind Kurt.

At its approach, Russell recognized the ghostly image. "Where am I?" The biker's ghost appeared confused.

"Niobrara County Morgue," Russell said. "The town of Van Tassell."

"Where the hell's that?"

"The middle of no one cares," Russell said. If Drago's ghost was still in the building, then there was no doubt it had been Russell that gnawed on the guy's corpse. He tried to recall the previous ghosts he'd encountered at the morgue. There had to be a dozen or so. Had he eaten those bodies, too? "Do you remember anything? After you . . . died?"

"Staring down a gun. Hitting floor. Nothing." Drago's expression was as empty as his insides.

"I'm Russell." He stopped short at extending his hand. "I'm sorry."

"What for?" Drago asked.

He leaned his back against the wall. "I'm the one who made you a ghost."

"Probably better then where I was headed." Drago floated by Russell and came to a halt at the front door. "Something evil is out there."

"I think it's my father," Russell said.

"Sucks to be you."

"You don't know the half of it." Russell cringed at the unintended pun. He approached and pressed an ear to the door. The townspeople beyond the morgue slept, blissfully ignorant. He cracked opened the front door and peered out the slit, listening. The stillness of the night was a welcome sight. The towering dark storm he'd noticed earlier appeared to be gone.

Cool air inflated Russell's lungs. Some of the businesses left a porch light on, their dim glow creating an erratic lit path on both sides of the street. Russell never understood why they wasted the electricity with everyone snoring in their beds or dozing on couches in drunken stupors. The night was typically his playground, but the shock of who he was lingered in his bones and he wondered if he'd ever recover.

A frigid gust of wind slammed into Russell's face at the same time a jackrabbit cut across the street beyond the front lawn. A coyote was in pursuit, on its mission to make the rabbit a midnight snack.

An earsplitting howl came from a nearby alley. The coyote may have been chasing the rabbit, but was something else stalking the coyote? Had Kurt gone outside in his werewolf form? Was it Doc Harvey? Russell slammed the door against the unknown.

"You're a basket of nerves," Drago said.

Russell walked halfway down the hall and paused. Why hadn't Doc returned? "Nana!"

For the first time in a while, fear held Russell in its grip. When his Death Eater emerged, as Nana implied, did he turn into an actual monster? Something grotesque? Why the blackouts? Was Nana right and he'd instinctively suppressed his inner demons? But with the threat of his father closing in, they'd encouraged him to eat these past few weeks. They'd created the full-fledged monster Nana had hoped to prevent.

"Nana!" he screamed with clenched fists at his sides. He looked at Drago, "I need answers!"

Drago disappeared with a whoosh. A moment later, he reappeared with Nana's translucent housecoat firmly in his ghostly grasp. She kicked and swung at him, but he deftly stayed out of her reach. A moment later, Nana calmed, and he set her adrift.

"No more lies," Russell said. "Spill. And I mean everything!"

"I suspected your father had something to do with your momma's death. But eventually he tracked you to the farm and murdered your grandpa when he lied to protect you. I wounded him, I hoped mortally. Praying, every night, he'd crawled off and died somewhere."

"How long have I been like this?" Russell yelled.

"Puberty hit and still I didn't see the signs. I hoped if I could get you to your fourteenth birthday, it might skip you altogether. But when Burt left you alone with my body, the smell of death must have been too pungent for you to ignore."

"If he's as dangerous as you claim, he'll kill everyone here," Russell said.

"These are good people," Nana said. "But they aren't saints. They have more than a few skeletons hanging in their closets."

"Meaning what?" Russell asked.

"Werewolves don't live on rats, boy. Gypsies dabble in dark magic. You figure out the rest."

The back-hall doors swung open. A large coyote entered ahead of Doc Harvey. The county mortician glanced at Russell, but his gaze rested on Nana.

"Did you come up with a plan?" she asked,

The coyote rose on its hind legs and by the time Russell blinked, he morphed into Sheriff Nighthorse. The deep crevices in the Shape Shifter's face gave him the appearance of being older than his sixty-plus years. His coal-black hair with white streaks was pulled back into a thick braid. The sheriff's badge gleamed on his chest.

Russell stared at him like it was the first time. Was there anyone else with supernatural powers in the town?

"We have a plan, but we can't leave the boy out of it," Sheriff Nighthorse said.

Nana rushed toward them. "Not the boy, you promised."

Russell didn't see how he could make a difference. He was nothing more than a supernatural vulture.

Kurt's head popped up from behind Doc Harvey's shoulder. "Russell's the one the homicidal maniac wants."

"It's obvious he's figured out Russell is here," Doc Harvey said. "Dusty was a warning."

"He's goading us," Sheriff Nighthorse said. "Evie's spell has him on the sidelines, but the boy can't hide in here forever."

"That or he'll find a way around my spells." Evie appeared behind Russell. He nearly jumped out of his skin, she gave him such a fright. But she turned and closed the front door behind her.

Kurt pushed between Doc Harvey and Sheriff Nighthorse. He strolled toward Russell with a smirk on his face. "That makes you our fishing bait, Russell Stover."

THE GROUP OF MEN, plus Evie, sat around the chipped linoleum table in the break room. They'd emptied the refrigerator of a week's worth of leftovers and sat hunched over their paper plates of fried chicken, gravy, lasagna, chicken salad and baked beans.

Russell's stomach lurched. He set down his fork, fighting the urge to pick up the drumstick and sink his teeth into it, ripping flesh from bone. He pushed his chair back and stared at the piece of meat like an addict resisting his next fix. It hadn't taken long for Russell to discover everyone could see and converse with Nana. He studied the group of people. "Why are you helping me?"

Evie set her cup of tea down with the manners of a southern belle and gave him a warm smile. "We're helping you because we love you, Russell."

"You're one of us," Doc Harvey said.

Sheriff Nighthorse took a bite of mashed potatoes. "We all ended up here, running from something."

"Or someone," Kurt said.

"Are there any other Death Eaters in town?" Russell asked.

"Your kind is extremely rare," Evie said. "That's why we were excited to have you."

"You've come in handy, cleaning up after us," Doc Harvey said.

"Except whenever my dinner was too measly." Kurt took a swig of his beer. "I had to fight you off a couple months ago."

"The real sheriff was dying of cancer," Doc Harvey said. "We needed someone to fill his shoes, to keep prying eyes away from the town."

Sheriff Nighthorse patted his chest. "Enter a new sheriff with a clean bill of health."

"Except for that ulcer of yours," Doc Harvey said.

Drago appeared in the room, eyeing the mound of fried chicken. He licked his lips. Russell felt sorry for the ghost. He rubbed his hands together, for warmth or comfort, he wasn't sure. His bones ached with a chill like none other. The drumming headache had returned. "What does my father want with me?"

"You have the one thing he doesn't," Nana said. "Youth. If he feasts on his offspring, he'll grow younger and be more invincible than ever. You're the first of his spawn to survive and come of age. Your mother hid you from him. After he killed her, your Papa and I protected you."

"But he can't feast on me if I'm not dead," Russell said.

"Keeping you alive has been a challenge." Sheriff Nighthorse set down his beer bottle a little too forcibly. It rattled the table.

Drago floated toward the refrigerator. He eyed Kurt's beer. "I can handle a fight."

"One ghost doesn't make an army," Sheriff Nighthorse said. "You managed to rid yourself of the others, Russell." Sheriff Nighthorse took a step toward Nana. "The problem with not understanding their importance."

Nana shrugged, then floated away.

Russell wandered out of the room and sat on the floor of his janitor's closet. Nana appeared next to him. "The day you died, and I set the fire. What was the strange dust devil?"

"A cyclone made of your father's captured souls. At first, I thought he sent them to suck the oxygen and extinguish the fire, but then they went after you," she said. "That's when I knew he'd stop at nothing to find you."

The horrific screams of his father's tortured souls from that day invaded Russell's thoughts. How many had his father feasted upon in his lifetime? How could he ever hope to outrun him? Would he eventually end up like his father?

RUSSELL STEPPED out into the night and stood on the front stoop of the morgue. It took everything he had to muster the courage to walk away from the security of the building. Evie's spell only extended to the edge of the fence, and the farther away from the structure, the more it weakened.

The crisp air rejuvenated Russell while he waited at the front edge of the yard with his head held high.

The scattered twinkling lights above the shop doors were beacons of hope in the quiet town he'd called home. He owed Doc Harvey everything for picking him up on a roadside, cleaning him up, and introducing him to the family who were eager to adopt a frail runaway.

It wasn't until tonight that Russell understood their acceptance of him. He could forgive Kurt the bullying, trying to snap him into a man and nurture what he needed to be. His role in this unique town of misfits, a scavenger gnawing on the scraps of their kill and keeping the circle of paranormal nature in balance.

It was time Russell faced his troubles. He couldn't allow his father to steal the souls of his friends. Russell imagined himself an old west sheriff, determine to rid his town of vermin.

Time passed, and still his father did not appear. Restlessness had set in and Russell considered leaving his post and joining the others inside the safety of the morgue.

A figure appeared at the end of the lane. From the silhouette, it was a tall man with broad shoulders, wearing what looked to be jeans, a light shirt, and a tan blazer. He strolled toward Russell with a stride oozing arrogance. It wasn't until he was a few yards away that he spoke.

"Do you know who I am?" he asked.

There was no white in his eyes, only ebony orbs that reflected the dim lights around them. His fingers curled like talons and his neck was unnaturally thick. According to Nana, the more his father killed and feasted on humans, the less human he became.

"You're my father," Russell said.

"A Death Eater on par with no one." He stopped and gave Russell a toothy smile. His tongue slipped in and out of his mouth. It was as long as a snake's, and forked at the end. "Are you here to lure me out into the open?" He raised his arms at his sides and turned around, then faced Russell again. "Here I am."

"Leave me and the others alone. Find your fountain of youth somewhere else," Russell said.

He took a step, but when Russell backed up, his father paused. "I'm tired of being regarded as a vulture among the creatures of the paranormal world," he said. "Once I consume you, I'll grow stronger, invincible. Then I'll emerge from the shadows and take my rightful place among them."

"In other words, you want what I've already found," Russell said.

"You're nothing but a servant, toiling to clean up their messes." His father's smile morphed into a sneer. "They don't respect you."

"Perhaps. But here, I'm loved. Nana loved me. Papa loved me." Russell forced a swallow past the lump in his throat. "My mother loved me. That's more than you ever had."

"You're the toy they keep around, play with and someday . . . will discard."

"I'm a child of the paranormal," Russell said. "Our kind has a place among the creatures. We serve the greater good. Now and always."

"You feasted on your grandmother. She's with you, isn't she?" His father took a step. "You drone on with the same preaching doctrine I grew to despise." He closed his eyes and inhaled, his chest expanded with the air of self-importance. "So be it." He dropped his head back and opened his mouth like a baby bird waiting to be fed. At the same time, he snapped his fingers.

A frigid blast of dark matter escaped his mouth and rose twenty feet into the air. It swirled upon itself creating the gray cyclone that had chased him into the gulley years before.

Russell clapped his hands over his ears at the deafening shrieks of hundreds of trapped souls. Their ghostly faces churning in the cyclone with screaming mouths.

A few of the ghosts broke free and rushed toward Russell. Drago appeared next to him. The biker issued a battle cry with swinging fists and rushed toward the advancing ghosts. His bodyguard landed solid punches as each spirit fell to either side. Part human shield and part wrecking ball, Drago paved a way for Russell to inch closer toward his father.

His father opened his eyes and turned a murderous gaze upon him. He waved his hands and the hovering cyclone lowered and advanced. Drago was sucked into the churning mass. The biker's ghost was whipped around a few times, then tossed out, landing at the far end of the street in a burst of light. He was gone.

The cyclone flicked its tip and knocked Russell across the yard. He landed hard against the base of the stoop. His thoughts whirled, and he found it impossible to breathe as the cyclone closed the gap, sucking oxygen out of the air and uprooting anything not tied down.

A waders-clad werewolf appeared on the stoop and grasped Russell, and at the same time sunk his claws into the post. The cyclone suction lifted Russell and the werewolf off the ground, and they flapped in the air like flags.

Nana's ghost swooped out the open door accompanied by Sheriff Nighthorse in the form of a massive coyote, but she immediately got sucked into the cyclone in the middle of the yard. "NO!" Russell tried to break free, but the werewolf hung on and snapped its fangs at him.

His father brought a fist down on the fence rail, breaking it into large slivers. He picked one up and threw it like a javelin. It struck the coyote in the chest and the animal collapsed.

A second werewolf leapt off the stoop and rushed at the base of the cyclone, disrupting its tether to the ground. The cyclone teetered and lost some its power, long enough for the first werewolf to drag Russell inside the mortuary. Evie shut the door and bolted it.

"We can't leave them out there. He'll kill them," Russell croaked while fighting to catch his breath. The waders-wearing werewolf took off toward the rear of the mortuary.

"He doesn't want them," Eve said. "It's you he's after. Come on." She grabbed Russell's arm and led him toward the back hall.

"Where are we going?" Russell demanded as they headed for the rear of the building.

"Your father is still in human form." She punched the handicapped button. "That's when he's at his most vulnerable." She pushed Russell into the autopsy room and locked him inside.

He pounded on the door. "Evie, don't. Let me out. You can't face him alone!"

"She has a few tricks of her own." Doc Harvey emerged from the shadows. Russell stood mesmerized as the Doc's clawed hands shrank in size and the hair around his neck and face slowly withdrew, as if absorbed by his skin.

"Why are you risking everything to keep me safe?" Russell said.

Doc's fangs shrunk. "Up till now, he's feasted on humans, but when he gets a taste of you, he'll turn to the paranormal creatures."

"Let us in!" came from the other side of the door. Doc opened it to admit Kurt and Evie dragging a wounded Sheriff Nighthorse. A piece of the split-rail fence protruded from the center of his chest. Blood mixed with spittle leaked from the corner of his mouth.

Doc dropped to his knees and examined the sheriff. He looked up at Evie and gave a subtle shake of his head. She brought the back of her hand to her mouth.

Sheriff Nighthorse grabbed Russell's shirt. "Eat me," he whispered. His eyes rolled back in his head and his hand fell limp to the floor.

"He's right," Doc Harvey said. "There's a chance you'll gain his power if you feast on him."

Three sets of eyes stared at Russell. "No way," he said and backed up.

"We're not just fighting for you, Russell," Evie said.

"Once he succeeds in gaining your youth, he'll be invincible," Kurt said.

"You can use Shape Shifting power to become any natural creature," Doc said. "It's the only way you'll have a fighting chance."

Kurt grabbed Russell and pulled him down, next to the dead sheriff. He waved his hand, sending the stench of death up toward Russell. The room swirled and melted into an endless void as Russell fought the effect it had on him.

Russell did everything he could to fight the urge and not change, but instinct, and the smell of a fresh body, was too powerful. He gave into the darkness.

THE CHILLED AIR stung Russell's cheeks. He rolled onto his back. The ceiling and walls were splattered in blood with intersecting loops and blotches. The stench of death permeated the room and Russell's stomach lurched. He took shallow breaths to stop the transformation from returning.

He drew his elbows back and pushed to sit, but he slipped on pools of blood that had soaked through his clothes.

Scattered bones littered the room, most stripped bare of muscle and tendon. Russell withdrew in horror at discovering four skulls. He rose on trembling legs and leaned against the examination table. No longer glistening steel, it was covered in bits of human carnage.

A note lay on top of the table. USE OUR POWER AND GO KILL THAT SON OF A BITCH.

"They sacrificed themselves," Nana said from the doorway. She and Drago floated alongside each other.

"It was a bloodbath," Drago said. "I've never seen anything like it."

"They kept death in the air to prevent you from turning human. They helped you the only way they could." Nana approached. "They bequeathed you their power."

Russell's lower lip quivered, and he bit down drawing blood, to make it stop. "The plan they told me, it was a lie. They tricked me."

Nana bobbed above the table. "You saw first-hand how powerful your father is. They had to trick you into understanding that their sacrifice was bigger than them."

"Not to me," Russell said.

"Then make it count," Nana urged. "You're the only one who can get close enough to your father." Her gaze fell to the scalpel resting next to the note.

A SLIVER of light appeared at the horizon as Russell walked out the front door of the mortuary. He ventured deeper into the yard. He had showered and put on fresh clothes, eliminating any clues of what had happened, and what he was about to do.

The split-rail fence had been upended and lay in scattered slivers across the lawn and parking lot. Why hadn't the piercing wails roused the townsfolk? Could only the supernatural hear the trapped souls? When they emerged on their way to work and errands, would they see the remnants of a tornado, thankful they'd slept through it?

Courage was all Russell had left in the world. His father had taken everything, and everyone, else.

"Show yourself, you coward," Russell yelled. If he aroused the living, he hoped they had enough wits to stay inside.

"The only coward is you." His father wandered out from behind Doc Harvey's truck. "Where are your friends? Your loved ones? Did they abandon you after all?"

"You have to kill me before you can gain my power," Russell said. He spread his arms. "So, come and get me." When his father dropped his head back, Russell chuckled. "You're the coward."

His father paused and leered at him. "I have an army! You have nothing."

Russell smirked. "If I'm so insignificant, why are you sending an army to do your dirty work." He took a step into the street, leaving Evie's sanctuary behind. "The all-powerful is afraid of a teenager."

His father's hands drew into tight fists, and he jerked his chin toward Russell. "I'm going to enjoy this." He rushed forward.

Every nerve in Russell's body came to life and images swirled in his thoughts. He focused on Sheriff Nighthorse's power and conjured a massive eagle. Gigantic wings unfurled, and a sharp beak elongated between his eyes. His sight was heightened, and the odor of his father's fear reached his nostrils. With a tremendous flap, Russell took flight and dipped long enough to rip at the man's shoulders with his talons.

His father fell to the ground with a roar. "You're going to die!"

You first, Russell shouted, but it came out as a thunderous squawk. He swooped down, skimming the main street and headed for the outskirts of town. There had been enough bloodshed. Russell wouldn't be responsible for more.

The cyclone formed at the edge of town and took off across the plains in pursuit, picking up speed, carried by the wail of trapped souls. Once he'd created enough distance, Russell touched down and shifted back into his human form. He shimmied down the slope, then shape shifted into a coyote and ran the length of a narrow, but steep gulley.

An earsplitting wail touched down overhead, but the cyclone lost power whenever it tried to enter. Russell had taken advantage of his birds-eye view on his approach and knew what he had to do.

The second he reached the narrowest stretch, he transformed into his human self, fell to the ground and rolled onto his back covering his face with his arms. Dust and dirt swirled about while the hovering cyclone sucked some of the oxygen from the surrounding air, but the gulley acted like a chimney and with every loss of air overhead, it was replenished from the channel.

After what seemed like an eternity, the cyclone lifted and lingered at the crest of the gulley. Russell coughed and sat up but didn't dare stand in case his father recalled it.

"You're smart," his father shouted from the above. "I'll give you that."

"Take after my mother." Russell rose to one knee. "Care to come down and finish this, face-to-face."

"Your shape shifter friend gave you his power." His father strolled along the cliff's edge. "What's to stop you from flying out of here?"

"I don't want to live my life looking over my shoulder," Russell said. He stood and looked up at his father. "Let's end this."

His father leapt off and landed on one knee at Russell's feet. By the time he brushed himself off and stood, Russell had conjured a massive werewolf.

Russell swung his arm and knocked his father against the gulley wall. With a shout, his father pushed off and dropped his head back, but Russell was on him, pinning him to the wall. He sunk a claw into the man's neck.

Blood gushed from his father's trachea. Russell dug his claws into his father's side and hung on to the thrashing man, lifting him off the ground.

At the fringe of Russell's vision, sunlight glinted off metal. His father buried a knife into Russell's abdomen. He howled and with the combined power of two wolves, ripped his father in half.

With the last of his strength, Russell withdrew the knife and dropped to his knees.

Frenzied by the spilt blood, his werewolf-self threw his head back and howled, but it was cut short by the stench of death. Russell grabbed his father's limp arm and bit down hard, scraping bone and ripping flesh from the limb.

The overhead cyclone slowed and teetered. A minute later, it dispersed across the ground. The wailing ceased. Darkness overtook Russell, and he fell to one side, clutching his father's corpse and tasting flesh.

Russell found a stream and washed off the blood. The icy water rejuvenated him, and he drank his fill.

He pressed his hand to his abdomen. The blade wasn't made of silver. The werewolf's self-healing powers had saved his life.

"You done good, boy," Nana said. She hovered above a rock on the opposite embankment.

"Except you're dead," he said.

"True, there is that." She pursed her blue lips.

"Everyone's dead." Russell struck the water and sent a wide spray across the stream.

A frigid hand rested on Russell's shoulder, and he shuddered. When he looked up, tears swelled and spilt onto his cheeks. He gulped back a sob. "Momma."

"I am so proud of you," she said. Her long hair fell across her cascading nightgown Even in ghostly form, she was more beautiful than he remembered.

"We all are." Papa's image appeared and floated beside Nana. His bald head reflected the sun and even in death, his belly fell over his coveralls. He threw an arm across Nana's shoulders and gave her a peck on her cheek. Her image shown brighter.

"How are you here?" Russell asked.

"When you ate your father, it freed us from his prison. We were no longer tied to him," his mother said.

"Did I trade your prison for mine?" he asked.

"Many of those trapped, chose to move on," Papa said.

"We're staying," his mother said softly. "With you."

Other ghosts appeared, crowding the embankment on both sides, Doc Harvey, Kurt, Evie, and Sheriff Nighthorse among them. From the looks of it, most of the trapped spirits left the confines of this world, but a few remained. Men and women of all ages, even a few children.

"You'll never be alone, my dear child," his mother said. "We're at your side, wherever you go."

"There's no place for me," Russell said. "I'm a monster."

Doc Harvey smiled. "We weren't the only ones out there, Russell. There are other paranormal communities. I'll point you in the right direction."

"And we've got your back," Evie said.

The edge of Kurt's mouth rose. "Bet on it, Russell Stover."

A NOTE FROM SUE DUFF

My Final Gift is my effort to put a spin on the paranormal world. There have been Death Eaters mentioned in literature prior to this, most notably by J.K. Rowling, but my Death Eater species takes its name quite literally. The fact that he discovers the monster in him at a time he's full of teenage angst, makes him an even more compelling character. I hope you've enjoyed my foray into the world of horror and will check out my other short stories and novels.

Thank you for reading MY FINAL GIFT. Here's a sneak peek at my fantasy/sci-fi series, The Weir Chronicles.

FADE TO BLACK

THE WEIR CHRONICLES: BOOK ONE

{1}

Ian DROPPED HIS ARMS, TOOK A STEP BACK, AND wedged himself into the upright crate. The door shut so close to his face that the heat from his breath bounced back carrying a whiff of sawdust with it. An itch caused him to twitch his nose and clench his teeth, willing the sneeze to stay at bay. Metal slid outside the wooden box, scratching the surface like an animal struggling to get to its prey. It stopped with a click of the pad-lock.

Outside, a swish and then a muted screech overhead pricked Ian's ears, a warning that his timing might have been off. Two of the massive swinging axes crossed each other on their sweeping pattern with the merest of contact. At the next approach, his upright prison would be in their direct path.

He blamed the sweltering space for the beads of sweat that bristled across his neck. Ian sensed as much as heard the overhead gear slip into the last notch a second before hundreds of gasps swept across the auditorium. Every muscle stiffened at the ready as he crossed his wrists. At the same time, he kicked the escape hatch lever with the toe of his boot.

Nothing happened.

Shit! Ian jammed his knee into his chest and stomped on the trapdoor as half a dozen axes shredded the panels surrounding him.

He tumbled down the hidden chute then came to a stop when his cheek smashed against the basement mat. A kaleidoscope of sparks sizzled behind his eyes. He rolled onto his back while remnants of the crate followed him down and floated in the air like confetti. The moment the overhead hatch closed, the audience's screams became muffled noise.

"Talk about cutting it close," Patrick said, leaning over him.

"I'm nearly sushi, and you're smiling." Ian gave in

to a groan as Patrick helped him to his feet. He paused long enough to catch his breath then started up the ladder. "I can't believe you climbed down here. Admit it; the illusion had you nervous."

"Why would I waste the energy?" Patrick touched the mat. His tone turned serious. "Ian, is this blood?"

"The price I pay for playing with knives."

"Keep that attitude and you won't make it to your twentieth birthday."

Ian climbed onto the stage and sidestepped the crew pushing the next prop into place. A shiver licked his spine. The cut on his hand stung when he swiped the drizzle of blood on his leather pants. Nestled in the thick folds of the curtain, he steadied the pounding in his chest and held his breath against the surging nausea. The occasional near misses taunted him, reminders that any semblance of control was the greatest illusion of all.

The rock music turned melodic and melted into the back-ground. A hush came over the room.

Three, two, one—up went his arms, bathed in blinding light right on cue. Ian's pulse quickened as he stepped forward for his favorite, and last, illusion of the night.

"Have you had enough?" he shouted, raising his arms higher.

"No!" the audience screamed.

Their enthusiasm triggered his grin and energized his spirit. "I might have one more surprise up my sleeve." He backed up as the curtains opened behind him, then he turned and leapt up onto the base supporting an enormous translucent sphere engulfed in crisscrossing spotlights.

The crowd broke into applause as it took in the magnitude of the device, which filled up the stage. The music's volume built, and the audience quieted in anticipation.

Ian scaled the sphere's outside ladder. He stood at the pinnacle and spread his arms wide. A flash of bright light and he appeared inside, clad in a black jumpsuit. The crowd went wild.

His identical twin assistants, Mara and Tara, stepped for-ward, their ivory costumes and snowy hair stark against the dark stage. They pushed the sphere's base in a slow clockwise rotation.

A motorized cycle stood like a patient steed in the bottom of the sphere. Ian straddled it and revved the engine. He drove the cycle around and around inside the structure, working the bike up and along its equator. The vibration coursed through his hands and legs. He increased the speed while emerald smoke drifted upward. He swerved and started to navigate in different directions. Pain shot into his arms and shoulders as the bike defied gravity. Bolts of blinding light erupted outward from the thickening cloud that engulfed him and the cycle.

The rock music rose above the engine noise. Ian and the bike dropped through the trapdoor inside the base and the cycle snapped into place just as the music ceased. The sphere's front panel dropped open. The gas dissipated.

Applause erupted at the illusion of an empty sphere but cut short at a deafening explosion. The crowd shrieked.

Ian, still astride the cycle, burst from the opening and flew through the air toward the audience. The unseen cable jerked him and the bike away in a blinding flash an instant before impact. A moment of stunned disbelief, and then the audience sprang to its feet, applauding wildly.

Whistles and catcalls intermixed with the familiar chant that had marked the last several months of his show. "Black! Black! Black!" rang through the auditorium. It fell into rhythm with the clapping.

The room darkened, as if giving the audience

what they asked for. Ian emerged from the hidden track. Concealed by thick smoke at the center of the landing, he sat on the cycle waiting. People in the orchestra section grabbed their seat backs and twisted around. The upper sections leaned forward.

The spotlight shone on the swirling mist, while the remainder of the auditorium waited in darkness. The opaque cloud dispersed. Ian's smile never reached his lips.

Images flashed through his mind. A graffiti-splattered wall—red coat sleeves, feminine hands flailing in defense—a masculine hand slashing toward them holding a knife. The image played in bits and pieces of motion and sound, as if seen on a television set receiving intermittent signals.

A new image arose, and with it, a searing sense of heat. A burning building as seen through a fireman's mask. Strain—lugging something heavy—then falling, weightless, glowing embers and shards of wood floating all around him.

Another. A car careening out of control. Terrified eyes in the rearview mirror, hands in a death grip on the steering wheel, jerking back and forth. The screech of steel brakes—impact—the car smashed into a guard rail. A moment of teetering—the car tilts—downward—looming concrete. Powerless, he could only watch.

The applause receded and Ian, coming out of his daze, picked up on the growing quiet in the auditorium. A reflexive smile touched his lips as he looked up and behind him, scanning the section between him and the girls.

The young woman was applauding, watching him with smiling eyes, the bright-red coat splayed across the seat behind her. Mara and Tara stood in the upper aisles waiting for his closing cue. He made fleeting eye contact with Mara then glanced back toward the woman. Mara followed his gaze and registered understanding with an almost imperceptible motion of her head.

"Patrons of all ages." Ian took a deep breath, trying to focus and regain a sense of his reality. Mara and Tara smiled, lifting their arms in unison while he continued. "Everyone at Fade to Black Productions thanks you for your support, your enthusiasm, and your outstanding energy during tonight's performance." He raised his arm. "Be safe and good night!"

Ian drew upon the earth's energy, and his chest filled with the intense cold of the magnetic field. The familiar tingling appeared. He shyfted the moment green smoke burst out of the floorboard nozzle and the bike lowered beneath him.

He reappeared in his dressing room.

Ian dropped his head back, welcoming the calm. Deep breaths purged the lingering tension of the visions while the audience's final round of applause faded in the distance.

The intercom on the wall came alive with a crackle. "I'm below looking at an empty bike on the track."

"I'm in my dressing room."

Click. Patrick broke the connection.

Ian flexed his neck while he peeled off his damp shirt then tossed it on the couch. He opened his hand and conjured a towel from his bathroom. He wiped the sweat from his face and dabbed at the clotted blood on his hand. Out in the hall, frantic footsteps approached.

Patrick burst inside and shut the door behind him. "You swore you wouldn't shyft during shows. You're lucky I was the only one down there."

"I had more visions."

"Visions, as in plural?" Patrick raked his fingers through his chocolate, cropped hair. You're killing me, Ian. Do the girls know?"

"They know," Ian said. "Tell Milo not to wait up. It's going to be a long night."

"I'll take care of things on this end." Patrick hesitated with his hand on the doorknob. "Ah, hell, I know better than to tell you to be careful." He exited as abruptly as he entered.

When Ian turned, he came face-to-face with the new publicity poster. His heartbeat returned to normal as he stared at the picture of himself on stage with his arms in the air, facing upward against a black background. He smiled, amused by the caption Patrick chose.

"In the world of illusions, there are many secrets . . ."

Ian had more than most.

{2}

RAYNE STUCK the rolled poster under her arm and buttoned her red coat as the crowd pushed its way toward the backstage door. She covered her ears against the adrenaline-driven chatter and focused on Zoe. Her friend's head bobbed above a gaggle of girls half her size. Rayne waved her over as the fans herded toward the barricades lined up behind the auditorium.

"I can't believe he doesn't sign autographs," she said when Zoe got within earshot.

"And to think, you got all decked out for nothing." Zoe scrunched her nose. "What's with all the makeup? And that dress."

"You can't borrow it," she said.

"Gal pal, it's not even my style."

She eyed Zoe's outfit. It looked like a cross between a punk rocker and a cheerleader. Her only true friend changed her hair color at least every other month. The current shade reminded her of kiwis.

Zoe peered over the crowd. "So, you hope to slip him your phone number or what?"

"Oh, please. You know why we're here."

"Says you. How many of his posters do you have?" Zoe nudged her shoulder.

Rayne's cheeks burned. She was grateful it was dark.

"Take a quick look around," Zoe said. "There're a few hopefuls in the surrounding gene pool. It'd be a shame to let that outfit go to waste."

"I don't care what you say. Ian Black looked at me," Rayne said. "I swear he did, right at the end."

"Puhleeze, the auditorium was darker than the make-out closet at Sigma Pi."

"What closet?" Rayne said.

The backstage door opened, and a man stepped outside. He looked around as if studying the crowd. "Who's the suit?" Zoe said.

"His manager, Patrick Langtree." Shorter than Rayne had imagined, this man was the face of Fade to Black Productions. "Ian rarely goes anywhere without him."

"Oh, you're on a first-name basis now?"

A moment later, the obsession of every girl out of diapers appeared in the doorway. Only his ebony hair and dark eyes hovered from over his manager's shoulder.

Screams and shouts ignited the crowd. The throng of fans swept toward the barricades while security guards stood at the alert. Rayne was wedged between two girls flashing smiles filled with glistening metal.

Ian waved. "Thanks for coming. I hope you enjoyed the show," then retreated back inside the building. The door shut and, without acknowledging the crowd, Patrick got into a parked limo. Its engine turned over, and the headlights lit up the barricades.

Rayne strained to see through the waving arms. Shrill adolescent screams split her eardrums. When the illusionist didn't reemerge, the screams morphed into chants: "Black, Black, Black."

The limo lit up from inside, a white glow spreading across the windows. The crowd quieted. A blinding flash. The illusionist sat on top of the idling car, clad in jeans and a dark blazer. Rayne squinted at him between globs floating in front of her eyes.

"Wow, they're full of special effects around here." Zoe rubbed her lids.

Ian waved for the few seconds it took the sunroof to slide open and then slipped down into the privacy of the limo. It drove off with a swarm of teenage girls scrambling after it.

"Oh give me a break, you'd think he was the last meal on earth," Rayne said.

"Take off those stilettos, and you could probably catch up in time for dessert."

"So much for my reconnaissance," Rayne said. "He didn't stick around at all."

"What part of never does public appearances confuses you?" Zoe rummaged around in her purse. "Since the object of your obsession has vanished, I vote we go to my dorm and make a tub of ice cream disappear." She pulled out her keys. "Come on, I'll give you a ride to your car."

"In this crowd?" Rayne said. "I could walk there faster."

"How far away are you parked?"

"A couple of blocks."

"Figures The Lion wouldn't grant early release." Zoe hit the remote and her car's lights flashed.

"The great Lionel Anderson had me doing filing all after-noon."

"Being a slave to your professor beats sitting in boring classes," Zoe said.

"Since when do you go?"

"Midterms might have something to do with it." Zoe regarded Rayne like a chastising mother. "Please rethink this insane plan of yours."

"There's more to Ian Black than trade secrets. I know it."

"If this blows up in your face, you could lose more than your work study." Zoe snatched the poster out of her hand. "I'm taking this hostage. That way I know you'll show up and won't blow me off. Someone's got to talk some sense into you."

"Seriously?" Rayne gripped her coat around her neck. "I bet you my new poster that I get to your place before you do."

"You're on."

Rayne headed out of the lot. She knew better than to take the shortcut to the next street over, but their race and her shivering shook away common sense along with her body heat.

Looming graffiti and the stench of urine greeted her when she turned into the alley. She looked down at her feet, breathed through her mouth, and kept moving. The enveloping silence magnified the drumming of her heartbeat and fell into rhythm with her muffled steps. She hugged herself while her wispy breaths led the way.

Metal scraping against brick sent a shiver up her spine. Rayne stopped cold. Instinct told her to flee, but the stilettos had their own agenda. She tripped and landed on her ass.

"Lucky me," a gruff voice said. "Unlucky you."

The man stood tucked away in the shadows of the building. She held out her purse with a trembling hand and then tossed it. "Take it, please, just take it and go," she said as the last five dollars she had to her name skidded to a stop at his feet.

He ignored it and stepped toward her. "Who says that's all I want?" The blade scraped against the brick building, dragging torment along with it. A streak of moonlight lit his face. He was smiling.

She kicked off the shoes and grabbed fists full of gravel, the only weapons within reach.

A green glow appeared behind her assailant as the knife slashed toward her. Rayne shrieked and threw the stones.

The man's body smashed against the brick building then dropped to the ground. He hollered and lashed out, but his knife connected with air.

She scanned the alley. Other than the two of them, it was empty. He got to his feet and came toward her. She scooted away. "Just take my purse and go."

"And miss all the fun?" He paused as if bracing himself for something. At a cat's screech, he glanced over his shoulder.

Emerald light splashed across his knife. A large object flew toward him like a Frisbee. The man fell hard beside her. The knife slid away. When he rose to his knees, he grabbed at his back. A weathered tire wobbled behind him before coming to a rest.

Rayne got to her feet then backed away. A trash can lid sailed through the air and smacked into her assailant. She spun around. A Dumpster blocked her path.

The man slammed into her from behind. Her forehead struck, and a star went nova in her head.

Bile burned her throat as Rayne's legs turned to mush. She gave in to the swirling lightshow.

{3}

Ian shyfted behind the assailant and struck the back of his head with a brick. The man fell motionless at his feet. The girls ran into the alley. "Tara, help her."

Tara knelt beside the girl. Mara headed for the man. "How bad is it?" Ian said.

"Her pulse is steady." Tara used a pen light to check her pupils.

Ian and Mara restrained the man with nylon ties.

"Whose turn is it?" Mara asked.

"Yours."

Mara pulled out her cell. "I need to report an assault."

A high-pitched squeal rang out at the end of the alley. A dark SUV with tinted windows pulled away from the curb, leaving behind a stench of burning rubber.

"We were being watched," Ian said.

Tara sprang to her feet. "How can you be so sure?"

"He took off without turning on his lights."

Mara drew her handgun. She headed to the end of the alley and looked up and down the street.

Ian studied their surroundings. "It's dark enough to provide us cover, even if they think they saw something."

"But your corona," Tara said.

"Flashes of green light, nothing more." Ian gestured toward Mara's gun. "Put that away. If someone wanted to jump us, they'd have done it by now." He bent over the unconscious man. "This doesn't feel random. Why were you so determined to get to her?" Ian's nerves prickled. Something wasn't right. "Tara, who is she?" He riffled through the man's pockets.

"Her name is Rayne Bevan," she said, holding up the girl's license.

Ian paused. The name felt familiar.

"He was just a perp, a maniac," Mara said.

"He's wearing clean, store-bought clothes. He wasn't looking for his next meal, or his next fix." Ian discovered the man's pockets were empty. "Why didn't he try to take off?" He bent over the girl. He hadn't failed a victim in a long time.

"It's not your fault she got hurt." Tara crouched next to him. "You saved her from something a lot worse."

Sirens bounced off the surrounding buildings, their wails growing louder by the second.

"Ian, we've got to go. She'll be all right. They'll take care of her." Tara tugged on his jacket.

When he stood up, an invisible punch slammed into the center of his rib cage. Stunned, he gasped. Slicing daggers and crushing pressure did battle deep in his chest.

ALSO BY SUE DUFF

The Weir Chronicles

Fade to Black

Masks and Mirrors

Sleight of Hand

Stack a Deck

Dim the Lights

Short Stories

Duo'vr *(TICK TOCK Anthology)*

A Mistake *(OFF BEAT Anthology)*

My Final Gift *(DEAD NIGHT Anthology)*

Adrift *(FALSE FACES Anthology)*

ABOUT SUE DUFF

Sue Duff was born in Chicago, IL but grew up in Phoenix, AZ. She dreamed of dragons and spaceships before she could read and combines Fantasy and SciFi in her breakout series, The Weir Chronicles. When she's not saving the world, one page at a time, she's walking her Great Dane, getting her hands dirty in the garden or cooking up something delicious in her kitchen. You can follow her online at sueduff.com

THE ESCAPE ROOM

A.G. HENLEY

60 MINUTES

Escape room.

It sounds like a horror movie title, but it's supposed to be fun, a game. You and your friends working as a group, using clues to solve the puzzles and escape the room before the hour runs out.

I bounce on my toes, full of nervous energy, as the four of us pack together in the darkened, musty room to wait for the hour to start. The girl who checked us in and showed us the lockers where we stowed our stuff closes the door behind us.

The escape room is cramped but cool; the air conditioner is pumping. Or maybe it's me. I'm always cold. I try to blanket my long blonde hair across my bare shoulders. I should've worn a hoodie over my tank top.

Baldwin checks his watch. Savannah, rainbow-haired with a new cartilage piercing in her left ear since graduation, laughs and punches Xavier in the arm after something he said. Xav turns to me.

"Are you excited, Zoey?"

I nod. "We're finally doing it!"

"I still don't get why you wanted to do this so bad." Savannah picks at something on her arm. "But I'm glad we're getting it over with."

"So I'll shut up about it?" I grin.

"No, so we have bragging rights when we get out in the fastest time," Baldwin says. We haven't been given any instructions yet, but he's already poking around the room like an amateur detective.

I don't care how fast we finish. To be honest, I'm not sure what about the escape room is so appealing to me. Maybe it's the thrill of being "locked" in a room, finding a way out while time ticks away, but with no actual risk. And it's something new. I'd lived in this town all my life, and nothing's *ever* new.

Savannah starts to say something else when a recorded, older male voice interrupts her. Baldwin shushes Sav, his eyes on the speaker in the upper corner of the room.

"Welcome to the Escape Room. We're pleased you've joined us tonight. Over the next hour, you'll have the chance to prevent a grisly murder using only the clues provided—and your intelligence."

"Aw, crap," Xav says. "If they want us to use our brains, the victim is screwed."

Baldwin hisses at him. "We're missing the instructions."

"Oh, oh, sorry," Xav whispers loudly. Savannah giggles.

"You are in the office of Doctor E.B. Perfidy. Doctor Perfidy is a surgeon *and* an amateur puzzle designer. Take a moment to look around. There are many puzzles in this room, some in plain sight, others not so obvious." The recording pauses.

We peer around the room. It holds a sagging couch, a desk sporting one of those ancient computers where the monitor is a square plastic box with the keyboard connected, and some rickety tables and chests holding a compass and a scale. A sharpened pencil lies innocently on the desk's hutch along with an old metal alarm clock, and a few dusty pictures hang askew on the wall. One is the Doctor's diploma from Central Midwest Medical School—wherever that is—and another is a picture of his wife. Or maybe his mother. Who knows? I don't see any puzzles. Are we talking the jigsaw variety?

"Doctor Perfidy himself is not here," Recorded Guy says.

"He better not be," Savannah says. "It would be super creepy if some old guy was hiding in the closet watching us the whole time."

"Shut up, Sav. There is no closet," Baldwin says.

"Ugh, it was a joke Baldy."

The voice goes on. "But in one hour, the doctor will return. And when he does, he will be murdered by an ex-patient with an, er, . . . *bone* . . . to pick." Recorded Guy snickers and coughs as if the pun was the funniest thing he'd ever said. "Unless *you* can prevent it." We snort at the fake seriousness that overtakes his voice. "If you solve all of the good Doctor's puzzles in time, you will be able to escape the room, warn him—"

"How good can he be if one of his patients wants to kill him?" Xavier asks. This time I tell him to be quiet.

"—And prevent the murders of innocent bystanders. People in the wrong place at the wrong time. People, perhaps . . . such as yourselves." We look at each other, eyes wide, and snort again.

"Do your best to solve Doctor Perfidy's puzzles on your own, but if you require assistance, you may ask your attendant for a hint. Only three hints are allowed, so use them wisely. The hour begins when I provide you the first clue. Other clues will follow . . . although not as quickly or easily as you might wish." He pauses and with a flourish says, "Good luck!"

"Good luck!" Savannah mocks the voice. Xav's bright answering smile draws my eye.

A faded orange Princeton T-shirt contrasts with his smooth, black skin. He's not going to Princeton in the fall, he's going to State with the rest of us, but he loves picking up random shirts at thrift stores for a few bucks apiece. Last week he had on a light pink one that said *Bon Appetit, Sucker*. We had no idea what that meant, but it cracked us up.

"New shirt, Xav?" I ask.

Baldwin glares at me. "Zoey, we have to listen for the clue. If we miss it, we're going to lose a hint asking the girl what it was."

I make a face. "You're taking this really seriously."

He frowns. "Russell came here with some friends a few months ago and got out in fifty-one minutes and thirty seconds."

"Are you sure he wasn't lying?" I ask.

Baldwin and his older brother Russell compete in everything. They're equally brainy, but Russell will say and do anything to show up Baldwin. Their youngest brother, Ford, is a genius and goes to a special school for geniuses. They gave up trying to be smarter than him years ago.

Russell, Baldwin, Ford. Yeah, their mother had a minor obsession with Hollywood leading men of the 80s and 90s.

My friend rolls his eyes and smoothes his light brown hair over the top of his head. He keeps it longish because it's already thinning. "I know when my brother's lying, Zoey."

Even if he didn't, he would claim to.

Recorded Guy is talking. "It's time to begin. Your first clue can be found . . . in the safe. Remember— the Doctor is counting on you!"

The metal alarm clock on the top shelf of the hutch goes off, and the hammering makes us jump. The room's too small to comfortably contain something so obnoxious.

After a full minute, Savannah yells, "Is that thing going to stop or is our first job to smash it until it does?"

As she says that, the alarm is replaced by a slightly less annoying ticking. Our hour has started.

I take my hands off my ears. "Okay, so we have to find the safe, I guess?"

"Everyone start looking," Baldwin says. "We already lost a minute to that damn alarm."

Xav salutes, and he and Savannah walk in opposite directions to check the tables and peek into corners, while Baldwin sits at the desk and stabs at the computer keyboard. I peer over his shoulder. A short, green blinking line appears on the black screen.

His fingers hover over the keyboard for a second before he types.

Who's trying to kill Doctor Perfidy?

"Shouldn't you ask where the safe is?" I ask.

He shrugs. "Doesn't hurt to find out who we're up against."

I can't tell you that. Each letter blinks into existence one by one.

"Wow, pretty responsive programming." He types in something new.

Where's the safe?

The ghostly green letters appear. *I can't tell you that.*

He grunts. "I spoke too soon." He types, *then what good are you?* The cursor blinks. No response. He slaps the side of the box.

I pat his shoulder. "Don't piss off the computer,

Baldwin. It might not help us later when we really need it. And relax, this is for fun."

He stalks off. I check the desk drawers, but they're all locked. Savannah messes with the compass, which must be glued or bolted to the little table it's on, because she can't pick it up. Xav rifles through a chest with three drawers in the corner. When no safe turns up right away, I sit on the slumping couch. The cushion is hard and lumpy. I shift over to find a more comfortable spot.

My eyes find the painting of the doctor's wife or whoever she is. She's carrying a thick, hardcover book. I get up and move closer to see the title: *Surgical Techniques Without Anesthesia*. Um, okay.

"I found it." Xav lifts a metal box out of the bottom drawer of the chest.

We crowd around him. The box has three rows of little black buttons on top. The first row has the numbers zero through nine printed on them, and the buttons below show the alphabet in order.

"Good job, Xav, that's gotta be it," I say.

"I'm so proud of you!" Savannah throws her arms around him and kisses him on the lips. Well, she misses a little and hits part lips, part cheek.

Baldwin and I exchange glances. The kiss was friendly but . . . flirty. Our group had an unwritten no-hooking-up rule. Not that everyone followed it. A familiar queasy feeling rolls through my stomach.

"Now we need a combination," Xavier says. "Anyone see a combination of numbers anywhere?"

Savannah points to the table behind us. "The compass has a little engraved plaque in front of it with a bunch of numbers on it. I thought they were those—what are they called—longitudes? But maybe it's the combination."

"Read the numbers to me," Xav says.

Savannah flips her hair back and leans over the compass. "22.02368."

Xavier pushes buttons. "Nope, not it."

"Okay, try this. 8.96007."

He shakes his head. "Damn. No."

"Try them both together." Savannah reads the two sets of numbers again, and he tries them without a break. We deflate when nothing happens.

"The numbers have to be a clue," I say.

Savannah jerks her thumb at the safe. "Just not for *this* puzzle."

"Should we ask for a hint?" Xavier eyes the intercom button on the desk that the girl pointed out to us before she left.

"We only get three." Baldwin's voice is strained. "We aren't going to waste one on the first puzzle."

"Well if we can't even get in the safe, then this will be a long freaking hour," Savannah says.

"Keep looking for a combination." Baldwin types something new on the computer keyboard.

The painting of the woman and her book catch my eye again. I pick out the letters of the book title using the safe's buttons. I shiver. Surgery without anesthesia? What kind of doctor studies that? I hope only the kind that doesn't have anesthesia available.

Xav watches me. "What'd you use?"

I straighten and tug my tank down over my jean shorts. "Never mind, it didn't work anyway."

"Tell us what you tried, so we don't do the same thing," Baldwin says.

"The book title." I point to the painting.

Xav pats my back. "Good idea, Zoo. I was looking for numbers."

Baldwin studies the picture. "Hold on. How did you spell *anesthesia*?"

I tell him, feeling my cheeks warm. My friends know I'm a terrible speller thanks to mild dyslexia, but it's still embarrassing.

"You missed a letter." He reads the word, emphasizing an *a* in the middle. "I think it's one of those weird, British spellings."

I say the letters to myself as I touch the

corresponding buttons, making sure to add the *a*. The top of the box springs open a few centimeters. Goosebumps spill down my arms as I lift the lid.

But when I see what's inside, I make a strangled sound and slam the top shut.

2

51 MINUTES

"WHAT IS IT, ZOO?"

Xavier sounds concerned but not shocked. So he didn't see it. I glance around. None of them did.

My heart pounding, I block the safe with my body, reach in, and slide the photo out as nonchalantly as I can, bending it inside my fist. Other prints slip around below my fingers. My friends press in to see what made me yell.

"Pictures?" Savannah reaches for the new photo on top and holds it up. Silence steals across the room —except for the ticking clock. We stare at the image. It's a shot of the four of us ... with Eric.

"What the hell?" Baldwin says.

I remember that night last summer. We were at the party at Sophia's house, standing behind the keg and holding Eric's legs as he did a keg stand. We were howling with laughter because although the photo doesn't show it clearly, beer was shooting out of his nose at that moment. In the picture, his skinny, pale legs stick out of shorts, his shirt has fallen around his chest showing a mostly hairless, flat stomach, and his floppy black hair hangs below his head.

Eric. Seeing him, us, makes my chest ache.

Savannah passes the photo to Baldwin and grabs the next. It's of Xavier and Eric in their baseball uniforms. They were on the school team until . . . Well, until Eric quit. The next shot is Sav and Eric sitting on a dock at the lake, legs dangling over the side, backs to the camera. They're ducking as Baldwin flips himself over them into the water to join Xav. I took that picture.

Savannah passes the photos to us one by one. Their faces are somber. I pretend to put my hand in the back pocket of my shorts, but really I'm slipping the picture I palmed into it. It slides easily out of my sweaty hand.

I won't show them this one. They wouldn't understand.

Savannah pulls out the last print. It's of Baldwin and Eric jumping on a trampoline in Eric's back yard when they were in sixth or seventh grade. We've been on that tramp a hundred times.

Xav, Sav, Baldy, Zoo, and Eric. We were the fab five.

Baldwin feels around inside the safe. "There's nothing else in here."

"You guys . . . how did they get those photos?" My voice shakes.

"They could have printed them off our Insta accounts. They had our names, right? Didn't you enter them online when you signed us up?" Xavier's trying to sound comforting, but his voice is too unsure to pull it off, and his eyes have the shifty look they get when he's worried.

"I guess . . . but are you sure all of these pictures were on there? Some are from before I had an account. And isn't that illegal? It's an invasion of our privacy." I touch my back pocket without thinking. I wouldn't want anyone else to see that picture. I'm one hundred percent positive I never posted it on any of my social media accounts.

"They were just shots of us doing stuff together. No big deal, Zoey. But what are we supposed to do with them?" Baldwin pushes the intercom button. "Hey! Hello? We need a hint."

Sav lifts an upturned hand to me. "Why does he get to decide when we get a hint?"

"Are you sure?" The attendant girl's voice is scratchy. I think it's supposed to sound old-timey, like a record player, but what she really sounds is bored. "Remember, you only have three."

"Yeah, I know, but we need one. The safe just had a bunch of photos in it."

"Right. Now look for a place to put them. It's . . . *hidden*."

We stare at the speaker.

"That's it?" Xavier says. "That's the hint?"

"That's it," the girl says.

"You're a big help." Savannah flips the speaker a bird.

"Something to put pictures in. Anyone seen anything like that?" Xav asks.

Baldwin searches like our lives really do depend on getting out of here. Savannah bumps into one of the tables with nothing on it, rattling it. She peeks behind the table and tugs on something. "Hey! There's a hidden compartment in here. But it's locked, too."

"Move over; let me see." Baldwin squeezes past her to see.

She huffs. "Excuse you."

"Good spot, Sav," Xavier says. She blows him a kiss.

"It needs a skeleton key," Baldwin says. "You know, one of those ones with the long skinny middle part."

Xavier hoots and pats the chest that had the safe in it. "I saw some in here. Except . . ."

Baldwin checks his watch. "What now?"

"There are a *lot* of them." Xav opens the top drawer of the chest. "See?"

We gather around. Inside the drawer is a cardboard box with dozens of skeleton keys of different shapes, sizes, and muted colors of gold, brass, and silver.

Savannah moans. "We aren't going to have to try them all, are we?"

I pick up a silver one and twist it. The letter B is written in black Sharpie on the hilt. I show the others.

Xav examines another. "This one has an L."

Savannah plucks one out. "Y."

I take a handful of keys. Some have letters on them; others are blank. "Maybe they make a word."

"There are no vowels. Where are the vowels?" Baldwin digs around in the box. "Wait, here's an A."

After a moment, Savannah picks up a silver key. "Another A."

"E." Xavier lays a black key beside the others on top of the chest. A and E are all we find.

I put the B beside the E. "B-E. Be . . . what?"

Savannah cocks her head and narrows her eyes. "There aren't that many *different* letters in here. They're repeats." She gathers them into piles. "B's. Y's. R's. T's. L's. And then the two A's and the E. We need to make a word that uses those letters."

We push the keys around in different combinations.

"*Tell*? *Tale*? *Ball*? *Bell*?" I say. "Has anyone seen a ball or a bell?"

"*Table*," Xavier says. "Maybe it's telling us to use a key to open that table."

"No shit, Xav," Savannah says. "We already knew that."

He looks hurt. "You found that secret compartment by accident. We could have tried to put the keys together first and not known about the table yet."

She puts a few keys in a row. "*Really*. As in, this is getting *really* old."

Baldwin shifts letters around. "Wait. I think Zoey had the beginning right." Slowly, he pulls keys forward to form a word. We stare at the word he's made. It uses all the letters.

B-E-T-R-A-Y- A-L.

I flush hot and choke for a minute as my mind strays to the picture I've hidden. *Tick, tick, tick.* Can't that freaking clock be stopped or at least the volume turned down?

Baldwin scoops up the keys and brings them to the hidden compartment. He puts one in the lock and turns it. It doesn't open, so he tries them in order.

He seems to take forever to insert each key, but as the L key turns in the lock, there's a loud click, and the door springs open. Baldwin reaches in and pulls something out. "Yes! A photo album."

Savannah throws her arms up, wiggling her fingers. "That's it. The girl said to put the photos *in* something."

A sharp pain at my temple makes me wince. I've been ignoring the headache and stomach rumblings coming on. I was running late after work, so I didn't have time for a proper meal. I should've brought a snack and my insulin kit in with me. Medications had to be allowed even if nothing else is.

Baldwin sets the album on the desk. It has a blue fake leather cover and four plastic slots on each page. A black and white picture is suspended in a slot on the first page—an older man with a white handlebar mustache and a wide smile carrying a black leather doctor's bag.

"The bad doctor, I presume." Xavier mimics Recorded Guy's cheesy voice.

Baldwin turns the page. An unsmiling woman wearing an old-fashioned long skirt, coat buttoned up to her neck, and pointy-toed boots stands with her hands together in front of her. Dark, smudgy marks stain the sides of the page.

"And maybe this is his . . . Mother?" Xav says.

"I don't think so." Baldwin turns another page. A third black and white photo shows a wary-looking little boy with shorts, a coat, and a cap with a brim. He could have stepped out of *Oliver Twist* or something. The same smudges mark this page, although not in the same places. The next page holds a picture of a middle-aged man. Black and white and still unsmiling. Same marks. "I think these are supposed to be his patients."

"Um, why is there blood on the edges of the pages?" Savannah asks.

Ice wiggles down my spine. "Blood?"

She points at the smudges. "Yeah, that's dried blood."

Baldwin flips past several more pages of the weird black and white photos to a blank page. Blank except for the blood.

"I guess we're supposed to put our pictures in here?" Xav's face twists with disgust.

"No," I say. "How will it even help solve the puzzle? What *is* this puzzle?"

Baldwin keeps flipping through the album. It has several blank pages, then at the back of the book, something is written in black Sharpie with more blood smeared around.

You will be weighed, measured, and found wanting.

My throat feels tight and swollen. The ridiculously loud ticking is making my headache worse.

"The scale." Baldwin points to the instrument. I'd almost forgotten it was there. Under the metal tray on top was a base with a glass face showing numbers, and fractions of numbers, up to ten. A thin needle rests at zero.

Baldwin closes the album and puts it on the scale. The arrow jumps to six pounds and four ounces. "Now let's put the pictures in the back. I'll bet that little bit of extra weight will do it."

"Do what?" I ask.

"I don't know. Let's find out. Give me the

pictures." He reaches out to Savannah, who's been holding them, but she shakes her head.

"You've gotten to do everything." Avoiding touching the bloody marks, she opens the book to the first blank page and inserts the picture of Eric in the keg stand. She turns the page and puts the lake picture in next. One by one, she slides the photos into open slots. I have a harder and harder time breathing as the pictures in her hand disappear into the book. She turns to the last page.

"Huh. There's one extra slot." She shuts the book and drops it on the scale. The needle swings to the right, pointing to a little less than six pounds, five ounces. Nothing happens.

I close my eyes. The last picture, the one in my pocket. I have to put it in the album so it will be heavy enough to trigger whatever happens next.

I'm not giving them that picture.

Xav touches my arm. "You okay, Zoo? You look kind of sick."

"It's really stuffy in here; I need to get some air. Maybe a drink of water." I head for the door and turn the handle. It won't turn. I try again. "The door's locked. Did the girl say she would lock it?"

"She locked us in?" Xav comes over and tries the door, putting some muscle into it.

I sink onto the couch. "I think my blood sugar is dropping."

My friends surround me. They know I don't say that if I don't mean it. Savannah digs in her pocket. "Here! I swiped a handful of Jolly Ranchers from the reception desk at work today when no one was looking." She holds out two, red and yellow. "Sorry, I ate the rest on the way over." I unwrap the candies and stick them in my mouth, letting the sugar dissolve on my tongue. Juice or soda would be better, but this will help.

"Thanks, Sav." I give her a grateful smile.

Baldwin hits the button on the desk. "Hey! Are you there? We need you to unlock the door right now. One of our friends isn't feeling well. She needs something to drink."

"I can't open it." A guy answers. His voice is record player scratchy like the girl's was.

"Who are you?" Baldwin looks as confused as I feel. The girl attendant didn't tell us she was leaving. The new guy doesn't answer. "Whatever. Whoever you are, I'm serious that someone's sick in here. She needs out. Come open the door."

Baldwin sounds completely in control. He's going to be amazing at adulting.

The guy responds. "I'm sorry, to open the door,

you have to solve the puzzles. Do you need a hint? If not, please continue with the game."

Baldwin turns red right up to his receding hairline. "Do *you* need a hint? How about we call your supervisor later and tell them you wouldn't let us out of here in an emergency?" He smiles at me.

Silence from the speaker. Baldwin slams the button several more times, while Xavier bangs on the door with his fist and yells. No one comes.

My heel taps against my flip-flop. I'd grabbed the latest start time I could for the escape room—eight o'clock—so we'd for sure be off work, and we hadn't seen anyone else in the lobby when the girl checked us in. We might be alone in here, except for the new jerk at the front desk.

"We should call someone," Savannah says. "But . . ."

"Yeah," I say.

We'd left our bags and cell phones in the lockers. I was stupid not to eat more, or at least to bring my insulin kit in with me, but I didn't think they would lock us in and not let us out.

"So . . . we're stuck in here," she says.

"Looks that way." Xavier sits next to me and takes my hand. "We need to solve these puzzles so we can get the hell out of here, get Zoey some food and her insulin, and kick *someone's* ass." He's joking, but he still has that worried look.

The room feels as if it's shrinking. My mouth is sandpaper. And all the while, the clock ticks, ticks, ticks.

3

37 MINUTES

I KNOW WHAT I HAVE TO DO TO SOLVE THE PUZZLE. Put the picture I'm hiding in the album.

Baldwin tried pushing on the album, causing the scale's needle to shoot up. Then he put a few keys on top of the album, but the change in weight didn't do anything either. It needed the fractional weight of the photo burning a hole in my back pocket. I'm sure of it, but as guilty as I feel about it, I won't give them the picture. I swallow, fighting the dryness in my mouth and throat, and glance at the clock. Almost twenty-five minutes have passed. Really?

Xavier and Savannah look frustrated. Baldwin runs his hands through his hair and curses.

"I know this is where the album's supposed to go.

Why isn't it working?" He reaches for the intercom button.

They're about to waste a hint—and more time. I'm not sure what's going on here, but I need out. With trembling fingers, I pull out the picture and press it against my thigh, protecting it. Protecting myself.

"Wait." My voice is low and shaky. "I have another photo to add to the album."

Baldwin glances at me, his finger retreating from the button. "Where was it? How'd you find it?"

I breathe deep. "It was on top of the pile when I opened the safe. But I . . . I didn't want any of you to see it."

They stare at me.

"Why were you hiding it?" Xavier's voice is gentle, but Savannah's eyes narrow as she waits for me to answer.

"Because it's private."

"Private? Why?" Baldwin says.

I shiver. "There's something none of you know. Eric and I . . . we were . . . together for a while last year."

"What?" Baldwin's mouth sags with shock.

Xavier raises an eyebrow. "*Together* together?"

Savannah stares hard at me, then at my hand, as if she can see the photo right through it.

I nod. "We wanted to keep our relationship to ourselves. We knew it would freak you guys out."

"You said you *were* together. When did you break up?" Savannah asks.

"In March."

"March. Right before—"

"*Yes.*" I say it louder and sharper than I mean to, then touch my stomach. I might puke.

"Damn, Zoey. Why didn't you tell us?" Baldwin sounds more curious than mad.

I wipe my eyes. "I didn't know what to do. I was angry with myself and felt awful for Eric because he had so many problems. But I couldn't be with him anymore. It was too hard. I couldn't stay with him after everything."

"You could have told us. We would've helped," Baldwin says. "We had no clue what sent him off the rails."

"I know, but I . . . felt so responsible. I thought you guys would blame me." I laugh bitterly. "And now I think I was right."

Xavier puts a hand on my arm. He smells like his signature Big Red cinnamon gum. "We aren't blaming you. It's just that none of us knew."

Baldwin nods. "You guys were stealth."

I try not to think about the last few months of school, when Eric fell apart, but the memories flood through me now.

The thing with Eric was a dream, sometimes amazing, sometimes nightmarish. And I was a dream version of myself, too. At school and at home, the same old Zoey. Diabetic. Fragile. Needy. With Eric, I was . . . powerful. It felt good. Until it didn't anymore.

I stand and hold out my hand, still clutching the print in my fist. "This picture. It was supposed to be for us. I don't know how it got here, but I think it has to go in the album."

A knowing smile sneaks across Savannah's face. She sticks the tip of her tongue out, showing her tongue ring. "Naked shots? *Zoo* is wilder than we knew."

My face steams. "Please don't look at it. Okay?"

Savannah reaches out. "No way. We wanna see."

Xav closes his hand around hers and gently presses it down. "Leave her alone, Savannah. Go on, Zoey."

After inserting the picture in the album, I shut the book and place it on the scale. As soon as it settles, a drawer in the desk shoots open. Savannah reaches in and drops something on the desk.

"Yuck."

Xavier examines the thing without touching it. "A scalpel?"

Savannah grimaces. "A scalpel covered in old blood? Gross. What are we supposed to do with *that*? Doctor Perfidy should be arrested. No anesthesia *and* he doesn't disinfect his shit?"

"Get a grip, Savannah. It's fake. A prop." But I notice Baldwin avoids the blood when he picks up the scalpel.

Is it fake? Is this a game? I'm starting to wonder. Who collected those photos? Who had that picture of Eric and me when even our closest friends didn't know about us? Shame burns through me, but I grit my teeth and focus. I need to get out of here.

"So what do we do with the scalpel?" I ask.

Xavier goes back to the three-drawer chest. "I saw something in here, shoved to the back. I wasn't sure what it was for . . . but . . . maybe . . ." He pulls out a doll and brings it over. She has messy blonde hair, one of those delicate but creepy white faces, and a faded pink dress with ruffles around the collar. It's also splashed with the fake blood.

Savannah pulls the doll's dress up a little.

"Someone used the scalpel on her already. She's a little Frankenstein—all cuts and stitches. That's so wrong." She offers it to Baldwin. "Here. You do it."

His lip curls as he takes the doll by the foot. "Do what?"

"Obviously we're supposed to cut her open with the scalpel."

His head jerks back. "I'm not cutting up a doll. Russell didn't tell me about any of this bizarre crap."

I nod. "The reviews didn't say anything about it, either. I never would have booked it if they had. I've heard of those scary escape rooms with zombies and things, but this was supposed to be a fun mystery one."

"Yeah, well. We have a scalpel, and a, um, patient." Savannah gestures to the doll. Frankly, it already looks dead. "So who's going to do it?"

Xavier, Baldwin, and I shake our heads.

She rolls her eyes. "Fine. It's just a freaky doll."

Baldwin lays the doll on the desk. Savannah snatches the scalpel, pulls the doll's dress up, and pokes the knife into the largest stitched cut in the doll's abdomen. Then she jams her fingers in the wound. Sav's expression is unfazed, but her shoulders are tight.

"Here." She drops the knife and throws a thin piece of paper toward Baldwin.

He reads it. "You did this."

My heart stutters. "What?"

He flutters the note. "That's what it says."

I reach for it. The words are typed with some numbers. *You did tHis.* "A password, maybe?"

"I didn't see anywhere to put a password when I messed with the computer before," Baldwin says.

"One way to find out," I say.

He touches a button on the keyboard, and the blinking green line appears. After a second, he types.

Do we need a password?

Letters appear one by one on the screen a line down. *Yes.*

Where do I put it?

Here. The line blinks. He types the password in.

Pictures flutter onto the screen. First, Xav, then Savannah, then Baldwin, and finally me. Mine is from seventh grade when I had bad skin and hair most of the way down my back. I'm rolling my eyes at the camera, one of my favorite pastimes that year.

Savannah's is from last year. She's pulling her tank top up, showing us her infected belly button ring with a sad face. In his picture, Xav is kicked back on Eric's couch holding an Xbox controller.

He's about sixteen, maybe. I've never seen that one. And Baldwin's is in the lunchroom at school in ninth grade, showing off his well-balanced plate with an exasperated expression. He's always been a healthy eater, and we've always given him shit for it.

It's like reliving memories of the last six years that we've been friends. Except Eric is missing from these photos.

I study the screen. I love these faces. We've been friends forever. But we're going to college. Everyone keeps telling us things will change. We'll make new friends, have new experiences, grow and change. I try not to think about it, but I know they're probably right. Eric already changed and not for the better.

Three letters in large font appear across the bottom of the screen, below our photographed smiles, frowns of concentration, and eye rolls.

R.I.P.

4

28 MINUTES

Savannah puffs out a breath. "Okay, this is officially no longer fun."

"Really, Sav? You're just now deciding that?" Baldwin's eyes are nailed to the screen.

"Shut up, Baldy. I'm scared. I want out of here." She bites on a nail with chipped black polish.

"Me, too," he says in a softer voice before jamming the button on the desk. "Okay, we're done here. We want out of this room. Now."

The speaker crackles, but the attendant doesn't say anything.

"What's your problem, man?" Baldwin says. "Let us out."

"No," the voice finally says.

"Why not?" Baldwin asks.

"Because you're in that room for a reason."

My friends look stunned.

"*What* reason?" Baldwin says.

The voice answers. "Are you stupid? Haven't you been paying attention to the clues?"

"It's a game. The clues don't mean anything."

"It's not a game. It's your life."

"What are you talking about?"

"You get out of that room in time, you live. You don't, and you die. Simple."

Simple. That word sends eels of emotions through my limbs. Shock, anticipation, fear. I jump off the couch and push the intercom button.

"Eric? Is that you?"

Everyone stares at me. The speaker is silent.

"Eric!"

Savannah comes to my side. When she speaks, her voice is soft. "Zoey, it's not Eric."

"How do you know?"

"You know how."

"He could have gotten a job here. That could be him out there." Sweat trickles down my shirt.

"It's not him." She gives me a little hug.

How can she be so sure Eric's not behind this?

Maybe he got out of the hospital early? They said this second stay would be a lot longer, given how messed up he was, but what if they were wrong? I glance at Baldwin and Xavier for support, but they wear identical doubtful expressions. No help there.

"Come sit down, Zoo." Sav leads me back to the couch. "You should rest."

I push away from her, but there's nowhere to go. The room is more claustrophobic than ever. And that clock won't. Stop. Ticking. I lean against the wall, close my eyes, and put my hands over my ears.

"I don't want to rest. I want to get the hell out of here!" My voice cracks at the end. I rush back and punch the intercom button. "Why are you doing this?"

Static answers me.

"Maybe this is part of the game?" Savannah's smoothing a section of her hair over and over. "Maybe we're supposed to freak out and think some asshole wants to kill us to make it harder to solve. We'll laugh about this later, right?"

"No, we won't. This isn't funny," I say.

She bites her lip. "I know it's not right now. I'm saying it *could* be. Maybe Russell didn't tell Baldwin what happened when they did the escape room because you have to sign something saying you won't tell other people what *really* happens."

"They can't do that," Xavier says. "Being scared can be dangerous for people." He eyes me, and I wonder how bad I look. "This isn't okay."

"Fine. I'm wrong. As usual." Savannah flicks something off her shirt.

"Whatever might be happening, we have a few choices. We can sit here and waste time arguing, or we can solve the next puzzle." Baldwin's face has calmed. He's always been the best of us under pressure.

"We don't even know what the next puzzle is." Xavier's hands are trembling.

"Then let's figure it out. What haven't we used yet in here?" Baldwin grabs the pencil off the desk.

"The compass," Savannah says.

"We used the longitude and latitude already," Xavier says.

I step away from the wall. "Wait, no we didn't, remember? The book title from the painting opened the safe."

"Latitudes and longitudes are for maps, not compasses," Baldwin says.

"Has anyone seen a map?" Savannah asks. No one answers. "Then maybe we need a hint."

I shake my head hard. "No. I don't want to talk to that guy. And we've used two of our hints. We should save the third."

"You don't have to talk to him; I will. And watch, I won't burn our last hint." She pushes the button. "Excuse me? Asshole? We *don't* need a hint. We just aren't sure what the next puzzle is. You know, since all we got from the last one was that we're going to die?" She winks at us.

The speaker cuts on. "Look at the computer screen."

The green line blinks at the end of *RIP*. Watching it makes me feel even sicker than before. Baldwin hits return on the keyboard, and a video starts.

It's the escape room, as dark and shadowy as it is now, but we aren't in it. The person holding the camera doesn't say anything as they pan across the couch, the desk, the scale, the table with the hidden door, the compass, the three-drawer chest, the paintings on the walls, the door. The video ends after about thirty seconds.

"O-kay. That was our next puzzle?" The pencil in Baldwin's hand taps furiously on the desk.

Savannah turns to scan the room. "There's something we're supposed to see in the video. Can we watch it again?" The screen is back on our pictures with the *RIP* below it, the cursor blinking. She presses return, and we watch the video a second time.

"Hold on, I think I saw something." She runs the video once more. As it shows the three-drawer chest, she jabs her finger at the screen. "There—that rectangle against the wall near the chest. See it? Maybe a big book?"

Xavier checks that corner. "Nothing here now, though."

"Then it's somewhere else. Everything else in the room is the same as in the video."

We spread out, checking inside drawers, behind and under furniture, even tugging on the paintings. I crouch down to look under the couch and wobble a little when I straighten.

Baldwin traps my arm. "Zoey, you're really pale. You should sit down."

Swallowing is hard with my parched throat. Why didn't I at least bring water? "I want to help."

"You can help by resting."

He leads me to the couch. It's frustrating that my friends sometimes treat me as if I'm breakable; but then again, they've seen me at my worst. The summer after eighth grade we went on a group camping trip to a state park with Baldwin's family, and I accidentally left my insulin out in the sun, spoiling it. His dad had to rush me to the hospital for treatment when my blood sugar spiked. It scared the crap out of everyone, including me.

I flop down and watch them search around the room, rifling through the doctor's stuff. Who is this guy? What's up with the bloody doll and scalpel and not using anesthesia?

I know Doctor Perfidy isn't real, but it's easier to think about the escape room's story than whoever might be out in that waiting area or why we've found our pictures around the room. Is it really part of the "fun" of escaping—making it more real? Or something else?

I think of the word the new attendant used. *Simple.* Eric said that constantly. If we were working on math homework—he was so good with numbers —he would show me how to do a problem, then say, *See? Simple.* When I was scared to swing out over the lake on the rope swing he'd made last summer, he went first. He'd come up from the water, shaking his dark head, and smiled his sweet smile. *Simple.*

And that night a few months ago, when he told me the reasons he'd always had a secret crush on me, he'd brushed my hair back, nuzzled my shoulder, and said, *It's simple, Zoey. I'm in love with you.*

It was too coincidental that the guy out there would say that. Not after the weird, personal things we'd found. This has something to do with Eric. It must. But what?

The stupid couch is hurting my butt. Putting my hand down to shift my weight over, I feel a hard lump. I lift the cushion up and find a worn leather document holder. I yelp with triumph and set it on the seat beside me. It's rectangular, like the shadowy thing in the video, with a flap over the top that's secured with one of those combination locks where you turn each wheel to the correct number. Everyone gathers around.

Xavier crouches to study the pouch. "We need four numbers."

"The longitude and latitude are too long." My breath is halting. "Try . . . try this." I recite a combination I know by heart.

He turns the little wheels to each number and pushes the button. The lock pops. He lifts the flap, retrieves a folded piece of paper, and opens it on the floor to reveal a map of our state.

"What were those numbers?" Savannah asks me.

My eyes stay on the map. "Eric's phone password."

With every passing minute, I'm more and more certain of three things. Eric's involved. This has to do with us breaking up. And it isn't going to end well.

5

16 MINUTES

LIKE ALL THE OTHER CRAP OWNED BY THE DOCTOR, THE map is old and sprinkled with dried blood.

"Read me the longitude and latitude," Xavier says. Baldwin does, and Xav makes an X on the map. The location is near our town, but the exactly spot isn't significant to me. I scoop up the leather folder and open it wide.

"Hang on." I pull out a blank piece of paper. No lines, no markings. Only plain computer paper. "Ugh. I'm sick of these clueless clues."

Xav takes it from me, turns it over, studies it. Then he holds it up to the paltry light. "Something's engraved here. Remember those grave rubbings we did in social studies class in middle school?"

He pushes the lead flat against the middle of the

paper and rubs it lightly back and forth. The others gather around him at the desk. I start to stand, but my head swims, and I sink back down. Not good. Sweat spreads under my arms, and my skin prickles. Definitely not good. I take several long breaths, trying to calm my body.

"What is it?" I ask when the pencil stops moving.

"A . . . riddle." Xav sounds choked as he reads it.

> *One who found me when I cried,*
> *One who stabbed me when I lied,*
> *One who took me to her bed,*
> *One who turned her pretty head.*
> *Four friends of mine—soon to die.*

I meet my friends' eyes, and for the first time see genuine fear. Xavier grimaces. Sav coughs and looks away. My heart jolts. Baldwin stalks to the door and punches it so hard I hear his knuckles crack.

Xavier's the first to speak. "Shit. Zoe was right. It's Eric out there."

Baldwin shakes his head, eyes closed as if that would keep him from hearing Xav. "I don't want to talk about him."

"Trust me, I don't either. But if we want out of here, we have to," I say. "The pictures are one thing; I guess someone else could have gathered them." Although, they couldn't have gotten the one of Eric and me unless he gave it to them. "But the password —and this—are another."

Baldwin knocks his other fist against the door to match the ticking of the damn clock.

Xavier presses out a corner the map. "Well, we know which one is me."

We nod.

Xav was the first to really worry about Eric, other than me. Right after I broke up with Eric, he stopped showing up for their baseball practices. Eric *loved* baseball. He was ditching school, too, although that wasn't so unusual. Whenever he did something to break school rules, I'd tell him they could still kick him out, but he didn't listen.

After Eric missed practice a second time, Xavier went looking for him. He was hanging out a town over with some people a few years older.

Eric had always been the risk taker, the one to try new stuff when the rest of us were chicken. He'd been the first to steal vodka from his parents' alcohol stash and beer from Baldwin's house. He'd bought weed from the guy who hung out in the park down the street from school most days after the final bell and resold it to other kids. But he hadn't told us—not even me—that he was using meth.

When Xav confronted him, Eric said he'd tried it a few times, but he was going to quit. Xav told him he'd keep it quiet until he got help. He looks tortured now.

"You didn't do anything wrong." Savannah wraps her arms around Xav, and he buries his face in her shoulder.

"I should've done something then, other than telling you guys. Told his parents straight off."

She squeezes him. "It wouldn't have done any good. He was too far gone."

"Well, it's no secret who stabbed him." Baldwin's face is red. "Xav could do anything, and Eric wouldn't get pissed. But *I* try to help, and I'm a dick."

I wince. "You had to do what you did. Don't blame yourself."

His blue eyes swim. "Why not? *He* does." He points at the poem.

One day, soon after Xav saw Eric using, Eric came to school high. He hit a teacher's car in the parking lot in front of a crowd of kids. Worried that he would hurt himself or someone else, Baldwin reported him to Mr. Goddard, the guidance counselor.

Baldwin tried to make sure Eric wouldn't get in trouble, but he was scared. We all were. Eric had never gotten this bad before. Mr. Goddard asked Eric if he had drugs in his car, and he stupidly lied and said no. When campus security searched it, he was expelled the next day and in the hospital by that night. That was late March, right before spring break.

Baldwin reads the page. "What about the next line? *One who took me to her bed.*"

Everyone looks at me. I'd already told them Eric and I were together, so this won't exactly come as a shock.

"I did."

I say the words at the exact same time as Savannah. Our eyes meet.

"You—" I stammer. "When ... did you ...?"

"A while ago."

"How long is a while ago?" Xavier looks pissed. Savannah slides her eyes to him and shakes her head a little, like, *don't start.* Something was definitely going on between them, then.

My brain feels clogged with lint. I know these four people—including Eric—better than anyone in the world outside of my family. How did I not know this?

Did they get together before we broke up? The last few months of the school year were a blur between trying to pass my classes, deciding I had to end things with him, and being so upset and worried about him when he was kicked out and hospitalized. Not to mention graduation.

"When?" Xavier's fists are curled.

She huffs and drops into the desk chair. "It's not really anyone's business."

Oh right, she wanted to see my private photo, but now this isn't anyone's business?

Xav glares at her. "I think it is."

Savannah bites her lip. She was the oldest of my friends, the girl I'd shared my secrets with over the years, had dozens of sleepovers and study sessions with. But we'd both changed, and I'm not sure how well I knew her anymore.

"Did you know I was with him?" I ask. "Did he tell you?"

She nods.

I swallow. "And were you with him after we broke up . . . or before?"

The room stills as we wait for an answer. I can feel the anger radiating off Xavier.

Her voice is soft when she speaks. "After. He came to my house really messed up one night, needing to talk. He'd just gotten out of the hospital the first time. His parents thought he'd used when he hadn't and kicked him out again. So he thought if they didn't believe him, then why not get high? But he felt like shit for relapsing. He stayed the night, and one thing led to another. He went back in the hospital a few weeks later, I think."

My throat clenches. "Have you seen him since?" When she shakes her head, I turn to the Xavier and Baldwin. "Has anyone seen him?" They haven't. I get up and stumble to the intercom button. "Eric, if you're out there, stop playing this ridiculous game and talk to us."

He wouldn't speak to me after I broke up with him, wouldn't respond to my texts. Other than sleeping with Savannah and getting hospitalized again, I don't know what he's been doing. Where his head is.

The silent speaker stares from the corner.

"I think we have to assume Zoey's the one who turned her pretty head," Baldwin says. "They were together for months, and she broke up with him. He was only with Sav one time."

She lifts her chin, her eyes defiant. "He texted after that, wanting to see me. But I said no."

I flinch. He never came back to me. Did he think

having sex with Savannah was the way to punish me? Or had he moved on? I've never been the jealous type, but Savannah *was* my best friend.

"Do we really think Eric is out there? That he planned all of this to screw with us?" Xavier's shoulders are slumped. "Do you think he'd take it this far?"

We're quiet for a minute, except for the clock.

"Yeah," Baldwin says. "I do."

Xav grabs a skeleton key and hurls it against the door. Even though it hit nowhere near her, Savannah cowers. I scoot to the edge of the couch and pick up the pencil. Eric means for us to see something on the bloody map.

"Xavier, after Eric ditched practice that day, you confronted him here, right?" I point at the town by ours. He nods, so I circle it. "Baldwin told Mr. Goddard about Eric hitting the car at school—here." I circle our town.

Savannah pokes her neighborhood, east of town. "Before any of you say something shitty, circle my house."

"And this is me." I draw another circle around the lake about a half hour south.

"That's not where your house is," Xav says.

"The lake was . . . special to us."

Right in the middle of the four circles is the mark Baldwin made earlier.

"What direction is that spot from here?" Xav moves to the table with the compass.

I tilt my head at the map. "Southwest?"

He fiddles with the instrument. "It won't turn. It's glued on or something." He grabs the table and shakes it. "But the top of this table is loose—"

With a grunt, he twists the entire tabletop to the southwest. He tugs on it until it lifts off. He reaches inside, pulls out a rectangular mirror in a thick metal frame about the size of a school desktop, and points to some words written in Sharpie at the bottom.

"The Family."

The clock ticks louder.

6

5 MINUTES

Xavier waves us over. "If it wants the family, we all need to be in the frame."

I try to stand, but my legs won't support me. After the shock of hearing that Savannah slept with Eric, I'm feeling even worse. My feet and hands are numb, I'm sick to my stomach, and my tongue is dried-out leather.

"I need sugar." My voice is a whisper.

My friends exchange worried glances.

"We'll bring the mirror to you." Xav carries it over and sits next to me on the couch. Savannah settles on my other side with Baldwin beside her. The boys hold the edges of the mirror and raise it in front of us.

None of us are smiling.

I look awful. I'm sweaty, my eyes are glassy, and my lips tremble. Without meaning to, I'm pulling away from Savannah, who looks as uncomfortable as I do.

We stare at ourselves. The boys start to let the mirror drop, but as it falls, our image ripples. Skulls replace our heads; bones appear where our necks, shoulders, and chests are. At the bottom of the mirror, words seem to drift up from within the glass.

Your time is up.

It's a trick mirror—I've seen them in haunted houses. Savannah would normally make a joke. *So dramatic.* But she doesn't speak. The clock ticks insistently.

"We must have missed something." Baldwin sounds shaken. "Keep looking around. There has to be something else that unlocks the door."

"The keys." Savannah bolts up, pushing the mirror away. "Could one unlock the door from the inside? Could we have missed it?"

She scatters them to the floor in her search. Baldwin yanks drawers all the way out of the chest and desk, while Xavier thrusts the leather document holder onto the scale muttering about how it might open something new.

I lie back on the couch, exhausted and clammy, and stare at the clock on the desk. Two minutes left.

What happens when the door does open? *Will* it open? It has to, right? This is a business. Whether it's a cleaning crew tonight or the manager tomorrow morning, someone will eventually come in here to reset the room for the next customers. What will they find? If we do get out, what will *we* find?

The hour hand on the clock points to nine o'clock, and the minute hand is almost to twelve, but the second hand isn't moving.

I point at the time; words are too hard to form.

Baldwin's eyes snap to the clock. He snatches it off the desk and turns it around.

"Damn him." He shows us a regular door key taped to the back.

"Go!" Xav yells.

Baldwin rips the key off and slams the clock back down. Without a functioning second hand, I don't know how close we're cutting it.

Savannah groans and hangs on to Xavier as Baldwin sprints to the door. With an effort, I stand and move beside my friends. Whatever happened before, whatever happens next, I want to be with them.

Baldwin sticks the key in the door handle and turns it.

The clock sounds one, final tick, then goes silent.

At the same time, something within the locking mechanism on the door handle clicks.

Recorded Guy shouts into the quiet room, making us jerk.

"Congratulations! You solved the last puzzle in time, saved Doctor Perfidy's life . . . and your own as well."

Baldwin cheers, Xavier pumps his fist, and Savannah and I clutch each other.

"Please exit the room and gather your belongings from the lockers. We hope you'll come again soon."

Savannah's face is a patchy red. "Not likely."

I lean on her as my vision blurs with tears. It was a cruel joke. Nothing else.

"C'mon, we've got to get Zoo some food and her insulin." Xavier takes my free arm to support me, and Baldwin throws the door open.

It's dark in the hall, as if the attendant already closed up shop and went home. But the locker area outside the escape room isn't empty.

A guy stands there, dark hair wild, his expression granite.

Eric.

I want to run to him, throw my arms around him, tell him I'm sorry, and I love him, even after we broke up, even after the last hour of torture.

Up until my vision narrows to the gun in his hand, the way it's shaking, and the one, final sound it makes as he pulls the trigger.

I came up with the idea for THE ESCAPE ROOM after, as you might expect, visiting one with some friends. I loved the little story world and mystery presented to us, the semi-creepy room filled with seemingly innocent objects, and the challenge of solving the puzzles. (For the record, our puzzles weren't splashed with blood, and no one threatened us. Good thing, too, because we didn't get out in time.) It occurred to me that we locked our cell phones up in lockers outside the room during that hour, along with everything else we brought. How many legitimate situations are there these days where you don't have access to a cellphone in an emergency? From there, it was a short jump to asking the central question: what might happen if four friends, each with their own secrets, were locked in an escape room together and couldn't get out?

Thank you for reading THE ESCAPE ROOM. Here's a sneak peek at THE SCOURGE, book one in my Brilliant Darkness series . . .

THE SCOURGE

BY A.G. HENLEY

I DUCK OUT OF THE STOREROOM AND INTO THE MAIN cavern, stepping carefully across the uneven floor. My fingers ache from being trailed along the frigid stone walls for hours. Rubbing my hands together to generate warmth has all the effect of kindling a fire with chips of ice.

My footfalls echo in the stillness as I move down the passage toward the mouth of the cave, counting my paces as I go. The sun pours in, diluting the darkness. I can barely tell light from dark, but I know I'm almost out when I hear Eland's voice. He never ventures in alone. He hates the caves almost as much as he fears the Scourge.

"Let's go, Fennel," he calls. "The celebration's about to start, and I'm starving. There's roasted boar and fresh bread, bean and potato stew, blackberry pie–"

I laugh. "Is your stomach all you think about?"

"No, I think about lots of other things."

"Really? Like what?" I reach out toward his voice.

Eland's hand, grimy from digging up vegetables and herbs in the garden, finds mine. Grimy or not, the warmth is a relief. "Like how we'll trounce the Lofties in the competitions tomorrow."

I can't help smiling at his confidence. This is his first year to compete. He and the other twelve-year-old boys have talked of little else for weeks. Everyone looks forward to the Summer Solstice celebration for the feast, the dancing, and the chance to beat the Lofties—with spear and knife, if not bow and arrow. It's a highlight of the year, so different from the solemn Winter Solstice when the Exchange takes place.

The shadows shift as we pass under the canopy of trees. I wrap my hand around Eland's sapling-thin arm—roots and creeping weeds on the forest floor have sent me sprawling more often than I want to remember. We reach the clearing, the heart of our community, where a bonfire sizzles and sputters to life. People shout to each other as they make their way down the paths from the gardens and the water hole, their work done for the day. The luscious fragrance of gardenia winds through the air. Someone must have strung garlands as decorations.

Our home, like those of all the other Groundlings, nestles into the embrace of the towering greenheart trees circling the clearing. Eland pushes open the door of our shelter. Aloe, my foster mother and his natural mother, calls to us from inside.

"Come in here, Eland . . . are you presentable? Comb your hair and be sure you clean the muck out of those fingernails. Fennel? Did you finish in the caves?"

I move to Aloe's side, where I know her outstretched arm will be, and take her hand in mine. Her skin is weathered but warm, like the surface of the enormous clay cooking pot in the clearing that never quite cools off. She smells of rosemary, from working in the herb garden, and something else I can only liken to the scraps of pre-Fall metal we sometimes come across in the forest.

"There's plenty of blankets and firewood, but we could probably use more salt meat," I tell her.

"We can store what's left of the boar after the celebration. We're fortunate the hunting party came across such a large one, and so near to home. The Council is pleased."

"When will they meet?"

"Soon. Sable and Adder want to perform the ceremony before the Lofties arrive."

Aloe will join the Groundling Council of Three tonight. One more reason to look up to her. Aloe is the most capable person I know. I was given to her as an infant to foster because she's Sightless, like me. She taught me to rely on myself first, and others only when absolutely necessary. Her guidance made my childhood much easier.

"Can't we come, Mother?" Eland says through clenched teeth. He's combing his hair, but it sounds like he's stripping the bark off a dead tree. "We want to see you accepted into the Three."

"Try not to make yourself bald, my love. And no, you can't. The acceptance is private, like all meetings of the Council." She kisses him, and her stick taps away toward the door.

"Congratulations, Aloe," I say. "We're proud of you."

"As I am of you both, my children. I'll meet you later, at the celebration."

Eland follows her out to check on the preparations, mucky fingernails forgotten. The scent of burning wood and roasting meat rushes into my nose and throat as he opens the door. It makes my mouth water. Animated voices burst through the clearing like startled birds.

I wash my face and hands with the water from our basin and sit on my bed, a low wooden pallet along the wall. I work my fingers through my hair—the same color as the fertile soil of the gardens, I'm told—and a thrill runs through me. I wonder if I'll be asked to dance tonight.

When a boy asks a girl my age, seventeen years, to dance at the Summer Solstice celebration, it usually means he's singled her out as his partner—for life, not just for the dance. My best friend, Callistemon, is convinced Bear will ask me. I'm not so sure. We've all been friends since childhood, and I haven't noticed any change in how he treats me. Calli says she can tell by the way he looks at me now. I laugh, but it bothers me that I can't see what she means for myself.

I don't know if Bear will ask me, and I'm even less sure what I'll say if he does. He's courageous and loyal, and there's no boy I like better. But . . . maybe I'm just not ready to partner. Aloe didn't until she was a few years older. I don't really remember her partner, Eland's father, but people say they were happy.

I take special care with my hair all the same, twisting it into thin braids here and there, and tucking in the fresh wild flowers Aloe left by the basin. It can't hurt to look my best.

Eland crashes back through the door to fetch me, and I follow him out. The bonfire blazes now. The heat isn't necessary on such a warm evening, but a fire makes everything more festive. A group across the clearing from our shelter howls with laughter. Hearing the musicians warming up sends another jolt of anticipation through my body. Calli calls to me as Eland scampers off. She's talking before I even sit down.

"You look so pretty, Fenn. I love how you fixed your hair! I'm so nervous . . . do you think anyone will ask us to dance? Well, I already know who's going to ask you."

I cringe. "*Shh,* he might hear you."

"Relax. He's way over by the roasting pit. Oh, who do you think will ask me? What if no one does? I'd be so embarrassed . . . but I hope it's not Cricket. He's so serious. And short."

"There are worse things than being short and serious . . . like being chronically unwashed." We both snicker. Hare, one of the boys our age, never picked up the habit of bathing regularly.

"No danger there. I heard Hare's asking Clover," Calli says.

"Clover? Really?" She's been saying she won't partner with anyone since we were about seven.

"That's what I heard," she says, and I don't doubt her. Gossip is rampant.

More people enter the clearing now, greeting each other with high spirits. Calli and I stand when Rose stops to say hello. Her tinkly voice reminds me of the wind chimes we made as children using pebbles and bits of shell dredged up from the water hole. We touch her tidy round belly, which is as firm and warm as a healthy newborn's cheek. Not long ago, Rose and Jackal exchanged bonding bands, the leather strips partners wear around their arms as a physical sign of their commitment to each other. Soon after, they announced she was expecting and due when the trees finally shed their leaves. It's a good time of year to give birth. The baby will be too young to be taken up in the Exchange, this winter at least.

"She's so lucky," Calli says as Jack leads Rose off. "They seem so happy."

"For now," I say.

"I can't stand the suspense! I want someone to ask me to dance and get it over with!"

"Why? It's not like you have your heart set on partnering with someone in particular."

"I don't want to be the only one not asked, you know?"

I do know, although I think I'm more willing to suffer the humiliation of not being asked than to agree to partner for life with whoever might feel like asking me today.

"Here comes *Beaarr*," Calli says, wickedness in her voice, "looks like he's bringing you an offering." I elbow her.

"I snuck a few slices of boar for you both. Be careful; it's still hot," Bear says, his voice a low and familiar rumble.

I blow on the meat and then test it out with a nibble. Delicious. Not many large animals are left on the forest floor, and hunting them is always a risk because of the Scourge, so boar's a special treat. The muscular texture and rich, smoky flavor evoke cherished memories of past feasts: music, dancing, rare carefree moments.

"Maybe this is your old friend, Fenn," Calli says, like she does every time we eat boar. I smile and agree, like I do every time she says it.

I was almost killed by an animal when we were about ten. We were playing hide-and-seek in the forest, and I was the seeker. Aloe made me memorize every path, bush, and tree in the area around our homes, so most of the time I could pinpoint where I was when we played. But on this day I was lost. As I wandered around hunting a familiar landmark, I heard what sounded like a gigantic boar snorting and charging toward me through the underbrush. Just before the animal reached me it squealed as if in pain and ran back the way it had come, leaving me shaking but alive. I don't know what caused it to turn around.

"So Bear, who will you ask to dance tonight?" Calli teases.

"Better worry about who's asking you," Bear says. "From what I hear, Cricket's got you in his sights. That is, if he can see you from way down there."

We laugh at Calli's tortured moans.

"Don't you think it's unfair that only boys can ask girls to dance?" I say. "Why can't it be the girls' choice for a change?"

"*Tradition,*" Calli says, in a high-pitched imitation of our teacher, Bream's, voice.

"Our *traditions* protect us from the Scourge," Bear says in the same voice. He leans closer to me, the smell of toasted wood clinging to his hair, and murmurs, "Who would you ask, if you had the choice?"

I chew a mouthful of meat to buy time. A voice bellows right above us, saving me from having to answer. It's Calli's father, Fox. He isn't one of the Three, but he's sure to be eventually, when Sable or Adder either die or become too infirm to do their duties.

"Ready for tomorrow, Bear?" Fox sounds like he's had one too many cups of the spiced wine.

"I still want to know," Bear whispers to me, before pushing himself to his feet. "We'll do our best," he says to Fox. "I hear the Lofties have a new crop of–"

"Rumors, rumors," Fox says. "Pay no attention. We have the advantage, as always."

Soon they're debating which shape of knife is best to use in the fights, or what spear grip will produce the most accurate throw. Other men join them to strategize. Some of the younger children run around us, shrieking with excitement. I lean back on my hands, enjoying the sounds of the people enjoying themselves.

"Fenn?" Calli says.

"*Hmm?*"

"Aren't you scared?"

I know what she's asking about. Now that Aloe joined the Three, I'll take over her duty and collect the water for our people when the Scourge comes again. I spend hours in the caves every day stocking the storeroom with supplies and food so we're ready, but we'll still need water. I shrug, feigning confidence. "Aloe says protection is the gift of our Sightlessness."

Which may be true, but I'm still terrified. The sighted say the creatures' bodies are open in patches, weeping pus and thick, dark blood. Their deformed faces are masks of horror. They roam the forests, reeking of festering flesh, consuming anything living. People who survive the attacks become flesh-eaters themselves. Death is better.

I'm supposed to be safe from the Scourge, like Aloe, but I haven't been tested. I will be soon. To hear the agony of their hunger, smell their disease, feel their hot breath on my skin . . . the idea fills me with dread and loathing. But Aloe has never shown her fear to others, and neither will I.

"I won't be completely alone, anyway. I'll have my Keeper," I say. Calli snorts. The Lofties say the Keeper's job is to kill flesh-eaters and deter other fleshies—our nickname for the Scourge—from getting too close to me. But everyone knows the Keeper's really there to ensure the Lofties get their share of the water while the Scourge is here. Secretly I'm just happy *someone* will be with me, even if it's a Lofty in the trees. "Aloe insists her Keeper was important."

"*Self*-important," Calli mutters. "And devious. Don't trust them, Fenn." We all know the fate of Groundlings who cross Lofties. They're found with arrows in their chests. Or in their backs. It doesn't happen often, but it happens.

There's a rustling, more deliberate than the wind, in the leafy branches above our heads. I sit up.

"What is it?" Calli asks.

"The Lofties are here."

The talking and shrieking abruptly cease. The clearing is silent except for the chattering of the fire. Fox finally speaks, sounding stiff and formal—and more sober than I expected.

"Welcome. Please join us."

The woman who answers sounds equally uncomfortable. "Thank you. We brought food to contribute to the feast."

"Our Council hasn't arrived yet . . . so I'll just say a few words in their absence." Fox clears his throat and continues in his best speechmaking voice—the one Calli and I have heard many times when we were in trouble. "Groundlings and Lofties come together once a year on this day to feast, to dance, and to engage in friendly competition." I smile as some of the boys quietly scoff at the word *friendly*. "The Summer Solstice celebration is a reminder that every year given to us since the Fall of Civilization is a blessing, something for us to treasure. It's a time to reflect on the year that has passed, and to anticipate the year that will be. We honor those who came before us, our elders, many of whom gave their lives to ensure we would have a future." He pauses. "And we offer a prayer of protection for those who come after us—our children, and our children's children. May they always be safe from the Scourge."

The Lofty woman responds to Fox's traditional words of welcome with their customary response. "We appreciate the hospitality of our Groundling neighbors. We too pray for peace and protection, and for a year of prosperity for all forest-dwellers."

A respectful silence follows, promptly broken by Bear's less-than-respectful whisper that the Lofties will need a prayer of protection tomorrow. Calli giggles.

"What are the Lofties doing?" I ask as conversations around the fire slowly start up again.

Bear answers. "Standing around, looking like they'd rather be anywhere else. As usual."

"It's kind of sad. They come to the Summer Solstice celebration every year, but they never seem to have any fun," Calli says.

"They should invite us up to their little nests if they aren't comfortable down here," Bear says. "Wouldn't kill 'em."

"Why do we bother to celebrate together, when we all keep to ourselves?" I ask. "We can do that anytime."

"*Tradition,*" Calli and Bear intone.

"Maybe it's time for a new tradition." I stand up, shaking out my skirt. "Where are they, exactly?"

"Over by my family's shelter," Calli says. "What are you doing, Fenn?"

Finding out who will be in those trees when the Scourge comes. I weave around the clusters of people, listening for voices I don't recognize. But I smell the Lofties before I hear them—the intense, slightly bitter resin of their homes, the greenheart trees.

"Welcome." My voice sounds too loud in my ears. "I'm Fennel. I'll be taking Aloe's place collecting water for our communities when the Scourge returns."

The Groundlings behind me fall silent again,

their stares heavy on my shoulders. A Lofty speaks, his voice deep and gravelly.

"Fennel, it's Shrike. Has Aloe joined the Council then?" Shrike is Aloe's Keeper. She doesn't talk about him much, but I've always gotten the sense she thinks well of him.

"She was accepted this evening. She should be here soon." I worry the pocket of my dress with my fingers. "Shrike, could I . . . I'd like to meet my Keeper."

There's silence, then someone moves toward me, crunching leaves under their feet.

"This is Peregrine," Shrike says.

I hold out my hand. It stays extended in front of me for what seems a very long time. I think of myself frozen that way, a welcoming statue found years in the future by someone who happens across the clearing. Embarrassed, but determined not to show it, I thrust my hand out even further.

A hand finally brushes mine. I can tell it belongs to a man. There are calluses on the ends of his long fingers. This Lofty smells different from the others, more like . . . honeysuckle. I liked playing around the honeysuckle in the garden as a child, avoiding the preoccupied bees and soaking in the sweet, sunny scent. It's the fragrance of summer.

"Hello, Fennel."

I'm surprised. I pictured my Keeper middle-aged, like Shrike, but this Lofty doesn't sound much older than me. And while his hand is rough, his voice isn't. It's quiet, almost melodious. More like the calls of the warblers that wake us each morning than the predatory screech of the falcon he's named for. All the Lofty men are named for birds, while the women have ridiculous names like Sunbeam, Dewdrop, and Mist.

"Though I don't wish the Scourge to return," Aloe says from behind me, "they will. It's good that you've met."

"Congratulations on your acceptance into the Three," Shrike says. "You'll serve your community well."

"Thank you," she says.

Aloe's voice is different, gentler, the voice she reserves for Eland. She has a bond with this Lofty. I wonder if I'll have a similar bond with my rough-handed, soft-voiced Keeper.

"So," I say to Peregrine, "were you chosen because you're a good hunter? Aloe says Shrike is deadly, as deadly as she's ever known a man to be."

"I can use a bow and arrow."

"Ha, don't let him fool you. Peree's one of our

best archers. We're counting on him tomorrow." Shrike sounds proud, like he's talking about his own son. Maybe he is. We don't know much about the Lofties.

Fox's voice booms across the clearing. "Come, eat, and let the dancing begin! We have some anxious boys here, waiting to find out if the girls they've had their eye on for the past year will dance with them." The crowd laughs, even a few of the Lofties. People all around the fire begin to talk normally again, and the music starts up. I'm relieved that the collective attention seems to have turned away from me.

I smile politely at my Keeper. "I'm sure we'll meet again, Peregrine, like Aloe said."

"Call me Peree. Everyone does."

I nod. "My friends call me Fenn."

The music starts up. I should go. Bear, or someone else, may be waiting to dance with me. Whether I want to or not. I turn away . . . and a mad idea grabs me.

Ask the Lofty to dance.

I hesitate. Is Aloe still nearby? Can she hear us? She's one of the Three now, tasked with managing our complicated relationship with the Lofties. There's no rule against dancing with them, but that's only because no one has ever tried. Aloe—not to mention the rest of my people—might be furious with me. I decide I don't care. At least I'll have made my own choice.

"Peree? Would you like to dance?" He doesn't say anything. I bite my bottom lip. "You know, dance? I'm not bad, really. I won't even step on your feet much."

"Lofties and Groundlings don't dance together."

"Why not?"

He's quiet again. "No idea. Tradition, I guess." I half expect him to say it in Bream's voice.

I hold my hand out, palm up this time, challenging him.

I never get an answer. Shrill birdcalls rip through the air—Lofty warning calls. The music dies, and for a moment the clearing is quiet. Then the screaming starts.

The Scourge is here.

Want to read more?
Get The Scourge on Amazon!

ALSO BY A.G. HENLEY

Love & Pets Romantic Comedy Series

The Problem with Pugs

Brilliant Darkness Series

The Scourge

The Defiance

The Fire Sisters

The Keeper (Short Story)

The Gatherer (Short Story)

Short Stories

Untimely *(TICK TOCK Anthology)*

Basil & Jade *(OFF BEAT Anthology)*

The Escape Room *(DEAD NIGHT Anthology)*

ABOUT A.G. HENLEY

A.G. Henley is a USA Today bestselling author of contemporary and fantasy novels and stories, including the Love & Pets romantic comedy series. The first book in her young adult Brilliant Darkness series, The Scourge, was a Library Journal Self-e Selection and a Next Generation Indie Book Award finalist. She's also a clinical psychologist, but she promises not to analyze you . . . much. You can follow her online at http://www.aghenley.com

THINGS THAT ARE
JUST TRUE

CORINNE O'FLYNN

THINGS THAT ARE JUST TRUE

I WAS NINE YEARS OLD WHEN THE DARKNESS CLAIMED my daddy. I watched it happen with my own two eyes. I know what you're thinking; I can see it in your face. But you can file that under the heading of *Things That Are Just True.*

It happened right over there, just across the other side of the cemetery. It was summertime and that magnolia tree was in full bloom. You can't tell it now, what with it being winter and all, but believe me when I say the smell of those flowers filled the air so thick it was as if the good Lord above had thrown open the Pearly Gates to welcome my grandpa, spilling the heavenly scent over his funeral like a blanket. I was just a kid back then, but God as my witness; I will never forget the smell of the flowers on that tree.

The funeral ended and everyone milled around —tossing flowers into the grave, and giving my daddy condolences as he stared down at my grandfather's coffin. Most people shook hands with the pastor from the next town over who had come to stand in for my father, who was a pastor himself but wasn't expected to preside over his own daddy's funeral. I was a shy child then, so I hung back, content to watch from a distance instead of being in the thick of any activity.

And that's when I saw it.

The darkness slithered right up out of the grave. It spread across the too-green sheet of fake grass covering the dirt pile they would later dump on top of Grandpa's coffin and tamp down flat. Eventually real grass would grow over it, leaving the world to think that Grandpa had always lived right there in his hole.

The darkness pooled like a smoky black cloud for a moment near the base of the dirt pile and then it moved in my direction. I remember holding my breath as it slinked across the top of the tidy neighboring graves, snaked unseen through the legs of the mourners, and covered a patch of dandelions as it coiled up over the tips of my newly shined shoes. One of my laces had come undone, and as my feet turned icy I worried if my untied laces had acted like an invitation, an open door to let the darkness get inside.

The night before, my daddy had shown me how to polish my leather shoes. He seemed nervous and a little distracted but soon fell into the familiar rhythm of daubing and buffing, daubing and buffing. I sat across the kitchen table from him, each of us with a shoe over one hand and an oily brush in the other. He showed me how to rub the black polish into the leather and buff it with a rag until it gleamed. The air in the room had filled with the tangy smell of gasoline and wax that was both delicious and sickening as he explained the procedure and told me with a wink to file that under the heading of *Things Every Man Should Know*.

The mourners continued to disperse from the graveside as the darkness wafted away from my cold, cold feet and found its way to my daddy. I watched and waited for it to pool around his shiny black shoes and turn his toes icy before moving on to someone else.

But instead, it stopped.

Then the darkness just seeped right up into him

as if his feet were a thirsty sponge and the darkness was a cool, wet puddle.

My father turned to me at that moment and smiled. It was a good smile, a real one with kindness and truth. But it was his eyes that stopped me cold. The dad-ness had gone from his eyes, replaced by something not-my-daddy.

Sometimes, when the light shines through glass just right, it breaks into slices of color so bright and pure you could almost forget about the darkness. And sometimes the darkness is so strong it conceals the true nature of everything so completely you could forget the light even exists. That was the kind of darkness I had felt in my feet back then and had seen in my daddy's eyes when he smiled at me all those years ago. You can file that under the heading of *Things I've Never Told Anyone.*

EVENTUALLY, life fell back into our normal rhythm and my focus moved from the increasingly distant and dream-like happenings with the darkness at Grandpa's funeral to counting down the last days of school and the delicious freedom of summer break that was almost in my grasp.

Mornings eased by with Mama waking me for breakfast and the three of us gathering in the kitchen as she served up her special blueberry pancakes with ham and grits. My daddy would wink at me from across the breakfast table as he asked for me to pass him the syrup or if I would like him to pour me some more orange juice—which I always did. Then we would clean up together and take care of a few morning chores before we got washed up to face the day. Daddy would give Mama a quick peck on the cheek and he'd walk me to school.

It was about this time that the first kid went missing.

She was ten years old; one year older than me, and she was last seen at the Sawbuck Rodeo and Livestock Show. That knowledge brought the event right into my mind. We'd been there at the rodeo that day, but I'd come down with an awful headache and Mama moved our blanket into the shade and made me lie down until it passed. News didn't reach us about the missing girl until the following morning. I remember being stupefied by the notion. How does a full-grown girl of ten years old go missing? Where exactly do missing people go?

This was before the days of milk cartons asking, *Have you seen me?* and Amber Alerts blaring across the airwaves. No, back then a missing child caused us kids to whisper and wonder while others spun tales of the boogeyman and evil spirits that kept all of us up at night clutching our bedclothes and for-sure-certain that every single noise was the creeper coming to snatch us from our beds. I spent many nights awake back then, praying for the dawn.

About a month later, the second kid went missing. This one was a boy from just over the Mulberry County line. Sheriff Hayman went door-to-door asking questions, piecing together the last movements of everybody in town on the off chance that someone had seen something.

Sheriff Hayman came by a lot during that time to sit on the porch with my daddy. Being that my daddy was the pastor, lots of people stopped by at all hours. Sometimes he sat with a neighbor who had hit upon hard times, and sometimes he invited a stranger seeking shelter or a bite to eat to sit and talk while Mama served up something warm to fill their bellies without making them feel like a beggar. Sometimes a member of our church used our porch as a confessional and revealed a crisis of faith. Sometimes it was what Mama called a Lonely Only looking for company.

It's just the way things were at our house. Visitors

would sit on the porch, rocking chairs creaking while they shared their worries and talked about the news. Mama always brought glasses of lemonade out for everyone. I was usually shooed away by the time the lemonade arrived. You can file that under the heading of *The Way Things Always Were.*

But not this time.

"You should stay, son." My daddy's voice moved through the evening air, soft and gentle as ever. He winked at Mama as she handed us all lemonades, my glass slippery with condensation. "Sheriff Hayman's going to want to talk to you as well."

The sheriff tipped his hat at me and I sat down on the porch swing, letting it glide just a little so as not to be disrespectful. My leg brushed against one of the large terra-cotta pots lining the porch. The pots overflowed with Mama's colorful pansies, which always seemed like angry, mustached faces.

Sheriff Hayman talked about the missing boy from Mulberry County. His name was Matthew Higgins, and he was seven years old with blond hair. He was an only child, like me. The sheriff asked us all to recreate the timeline from the past weekend, with special attention to the Strawberry Festival last Sunday afternoon. "You never know what you know," the sheriff explained. "We see all kinds of things and lock them away up here." He tapped his temple under his wide-brimmed sheriff's hat. "Most likely it'll end up that the boy wandered too far into the woods and lost track of time, but with the Larsen girl still missing over in Sawbuck Village . . ."

I wasn't able to help with Sheriff Hayman's investigation; I couldn't remember much about the afternoon at the Strawberry Festival. I'd seen some friends from school there with their families, but as far as I knew, those people were all safe and sound at home.

THE NEXT WEEK was the last week of school. As usual, my daddy walked with me and we made our way to town where my school was kitty-corner from my father's church. We stopped at the crosswalk to wait for the light. Kids pooled around us as the traffic slowed, and then the crowd spread out as we got the all-clear to cross. I was all the way on the other side of the street when I realized my daddy was no longer beside me. I turned and found him still on the opposite corner.

He stared in front of him, eyes a little hooded as if he'd been mesmerized. Kids bumped and moved around him like he was a boulder in a creek, crowding on the corner as they hurried to make the light. He didn't stop staring, and he didn't move.

My heart raced. Was something wrong? I looked over my shoulder to see what he might be looking at, but it was just a regular morning in front of school with loads of kids and parents and teachers heading this way and that, but mostly standing around waiting for the bell.

"Daddy?" I called.

He didn't respond. He didn't seem to have heard me. So I waited for the last of the cars to pass and ran back to my father's side. He stared straight ahead, unblinking, as if in a trance. His breathing was more like a hiss from the back of his throat. His fists were clenched so tight at his sides they trembled.

I turned again and tried to follow his gaze, but I wasn't very tall, even among the other students in my fourth grade class, and I couldn't see anything over the gaggle of kids milling about in front of the school.

Danny Parsons caught my eye and waved hello. I waved back and shifted my gaze to see Anthony Martin say something to his sister, Cici, who nodded and walked off, sending her golden ponytail bobbing in the sunlight. A pair of squirrels darted across a low branch and the birds sang from the trees. It was just a plain old regular morning in front of the school.

I tugged on Daddy's wrist. "Are you all right? Should I run home and get Mama?"

He tilted his head to me but kept his eyes looking forward, watching whatever it was that had stolen his attention. I could swear I saw a hint of the darkness move behind his eyes just then. I swallowed hard and I turned again to follow his gaze. Cici Martin hurried to meet up with a friend. She turned and nodded, sending her shiny ponytail bobbing.

Ice moved through me from my toes all the way up and landed like a steely ball in my belly. Was he watching Cici?

"Daddy?" I tried to keep my voice from wavering.

He blinked, and his eyes cleared as a smile spread across his face. "Ain't no thing, son. Ain't no thing." He mussed the hair on top of my head in reassurance, and just like that, the tension broke and floated away on the morning breeze. "Let's get you to school, now."

The rest of the school day rolled by like any other, except the class work was light and everyone had their sights on summer. Even the teachers let us out for lunch recess early and called us back in late. I remember being out in the schoolyard and spotting my daddy on the church steps across the street. He stood facing the school with his hands on his hips, watching us kids. I waved at him, but he didn't wave back. The sun was noonday bright and he probably couldn't see me.

By the afternoon bell, I had forgotten completely about Daddy's spell that morning, and by the end of the week, it was a distant memory.

On the last day before summer break, the school carnival brought out the whole town. There was music, games, and potluck tables spread out from the front steps all the way to the monkey bars.

Mrs. Simms made dozens of her famous fruit pies, one of which I may or may not have put my finger into. Mayor Childers came and talked to us about being good citizens of Fern Leaf and not to get into any mischief over the summer vacation. And Sheriff Hayman told us all to be safe and aware and use the buddy system whenever we were outdoors. Even Daddy came to share about the fun activities going on at the church all summer long, starting the very next week with vacation Bible school.

Nobody noticed when it was exactly that Cici Martin disappeared.

One minute she was playing a game of kick-the-can with a bunch of us kids, hiding and chasing, and hiding again, and then she seemed to go hiding where nobody could find her.

At first, us kids figured she had simply found the best hiding spot. But before long, after everyone called for her, spreading out and shouting her name over and over, her mama melted like a pat of butter on the griddle, her tears flowing for all to see.

She was just gone. Since the whole town was there, we organized into search parties and fanned out from the school. Everyone tried to *recreate the timeline* as Sheriff Hayman said, closing our eyes and walking back through the afternoon in our minds. But nobody could agree on the last time anyone saw Cici. I remember I closed my eyes tight and tried to my hardest to remember but all I could see in my mind's eye was her golden ponytail shining in the sun.

Hadn't she been playing in the last round of our game? Behind my closed eyes I tried to picture her as she ran to hide after someone had kicked the can. Was that the last time I'd seen her? Or, had she taken a break to have something to eat? Was she among the group of kids who had been sitting in the shade eating Sno-Cones with Tammy Parker and the other fourth graders?

Cici's brother, Anthony, wandered around the schoolyard like a lost puppy. He and Cici were twins. People say twins have a real tight bond; even closer than that of a regular sibling. As an only child myself, I could only speculate about what that meant, but it sounded like they were as close as close could be. I wondered if there were ever cases where a twin was able to locate their missing sibling using their special twin senses.

Anthony and Cici's daddy, Mr. Martin, trudged through the woods with a search party, as if Cici had somehow gotten lost in her own home town. I didn't think *that* made any sense at all; searching right here in the woods where we all grew up. But I kept that to myself, filed under the heading of *Thoughts That Wouldn't Help Anybody*.

Mrs. Martin stayed in the schoolyard so someone would be there when Cici returned.

But she didn't return.

Not even when the streetlights came on. Pretty soon everyone was counting Cici as a lost child. It was chilling when I heard it spoken aloud for the first time like it was official. Cici Martin was *Missing*.

Missing.

The word sent a chill of terror and awareness down my spine as I realized my world had stopped being the same as it had always been. It was like a story ripped from the pages of one of my *Incredible Science Fiction* comic books where the world had broken into two pieces that forked off and there were now two worlds careening off in different directions at the same time. On one side was the old world— the world where Cici and Anthony Martin and all us kids went home to supper and got tucked into bed where we had dreams full of summer vacation and ice cream socials.

The other side was this world—it looked pretty much the same, but everything was suddenly covered in the slightest little shadow. On this side, Cici Martin was the third missing child in the past two-and-a-half-months. On this side, I stood watching as the old world faded away into the distance and our small town was changed forever.

I tried to think what my parents would do if I turned up missing. I scanned the schoolyard until I spotted Mama and found her watching over a bunch of little ones near the sandbox while their parents kept on with the searches. That was just like Mama; making sure things stayed safe and sound at home while the rest of the world went on about its business.

My mama was a praying woman, and I saw her cross herself, her lips moving as she said a prayer over all those little children in her care.

Behind the school, in the thick grass of the baseball outfield, my daddy stood, watching the waving flashlights move in the distance as the search party walked a line through the woods again. He stood ramrod straight, with his hands at his sides, his fists clenched tight. I imagined his hands trembling like they did that morning in front of the school.

Adrenaline zinged through my body as I watched him. He didn't move a hair, didn't blink his eyes. I didn't have to be close to him to imagine the hissing sound his breath was probably making. But this time, darkness swarmed around his head like a cloud of midges, circling and weaving in a crazy dance. Then, like he had that morning only a few days ago, he blinked and turned, as if sensing my stare.

He walked over to me as he wiped the sweat from his forehead with a rag from his pocket. The darkness continued to swarm around his head though he didn't seem to take any notice. Couldn't he see it? Didn't it make his skin crawl with the thought of breathing in a cloud of tiny bugs?

As he grew closer, my feet turned stone cold, and I was reminded of that morning at my grandpa's funeral when the darkness had slithered up out of the grave hole and tickled the tips of my shoes.

It was in that moment that I knew. I knew it like I knew the sun would rise in the east tomorrow morning and set tomorrow evening in the west. I knew it like I knew the taste of Mama's praline pie and the smell of Daddy's coffee brewing in the kitchen every morning. I knew it like I knew what I had seen that day in the cemetery when the darkness had been sucked up into my father.

I knew it. The darkness had taken Cici Martin.

The darkness knew where she was. But the darkness was inside my daddy, and that was a problem the proportions of which my nine-year-old self couldn't really fathom back then. I felt paralyzed —boxed in—and I knew I couldn't tell a living soul. I didn't have to be told that I could file that under the heading of *Things I Wasn't Supposed To Know.*

I DIDN'T SLEEP a wink that night. I lay awake

watching the wedge of moonlight stretch across the ceiling of my bedroom. My mind spun with wondering about Cici and her sunshine hair and about my father and the black cloud and the darkness.

It was just before dawn when my bedroom door opened and my father sat on the foot of my bed. He grabbed my foot and shook it to wake me though I hadn't been sleeping; I'd only closed my eyes to pretend for his sake.

"Son? I would like to talk to you about something." His breathing was easy and normal, and his voice was gentle as always. "Wake up, son. This is something important."

I rolled over and rubbed the pretend sleepiness from my face. There was no cloud around my daddy's head, no darkness behind his eyes. He was just my daddy, through and through. My heart filled with relief.

He cleared his throat. "I was fourteen years old when my granddaddy died. He was a good man, a preacher like me and like my father too. He founded the First Baptist Church of Bayou Gulch over in Beaumont."

I nodded. "I know, Daddy. You tell Mama and me about him whenever we drive through Beaumont on the way to the lake. Same as when we pass by Mount Faith Baptist in Picayune that was founded by Grandpa."

He mussed my hair and smiled. "That's right. Our family has founded churches up and down and all across the good state of Mississippi. It's what we do, son. We bring the good Lord above into the hearts and minds of the people down here on earth. It's our saving grace, and our solemn duty."

I swelled with pride at the legacy I would inherit. "And maybe one day I'll be able to drive my family by Fern Leaf Baptist and tell all about you, Daddy."

He laughed softly and grew somber. "That's how it ought to be, son. Rightly so. You're a good boy." He drew in his breath and let it out in a rush. "Well, when my granddaddy died, after the funeral was over, I had an experience. That's what I would like to talk with you about, son."

I clutched my blanket to my chest, my heart thrumming inside me. My mind traveled back to the funeral of my own grandpa and the way the darkness slithered out of the grave hole.

My daddy clasped his hands together and placed them in his lap. "I didn't know until after, but it was something that my own daddy experienced and his daddy before him, and on and on." He shifted a little bit on the bottom of my bed as if he were uncomfortable sharing. I wanted to tell him to stop. That I didn't need to hear this story. I wanted him to know that I could be trusted with his secret.

But he carried on. "And, well, I suspect something similar happened to you at Grandpa's funeral. Do you know what it is that I am talking about?" He gripped my toes and squeezed.

I stared at my daddy's hands holding my feet through the blankets. My toes, which had been icy cold ever since that day at Grandpa's funeral, flushed with heat under his touch. I sighed with the delicious feeling of warmth I hadn't felt since that day in the cemetery when the darkness touched me. It was as if somebody had switched on the sun underneath my blankets. It felt wonderful.

"Mmm hmm." Daddy nodded at my reaction. "As I suspected." He let go of my feet and ran his fingers through his hair.

The warmth left me in an instant. I was overcome with a bereavement of sorts; I wanted that warmth back. I wanted him to turn it back on.

But he didn't. He just continued telling his story. "Well, son, I'm going to share something with you. It's the same something that my daddy shared with me and that his daddy shared with him when the time came. I expect you already know this, but what I'm about to tell you should be filed under the heading of *Things Nobody Can Ever Know.*"

W HEN I ARRIVED at the breakfast table the following morning, I was a changed man. I was still all of nine years old, but as I sat across the table from my father, I looked him in the eye and saw the threads of understanding cross between us. We were joined now by his little secret—now our little secret—one that we would both take to our graves.

He confessed to me that he had taken Cici for the darkness. He had said the words straight out. I couldn't believe it, and at the same time, I knew that it was true. Cici was being held captive by my father. Captive for the darkness. He wouldn't tell me where, and he wouldn't tell me why, but he assured me that he was doing God's own work, and that this was the only way.

"The only way for what?" I'd asked, still very much confused and afraid, but also filled with a sense of wonder and deep understanding that I couldn't quite explain. Perhaps it was the surety in his eyes and in his voice. Perhaps it was the fact that

I'd been there; I'd seen when the darkness had taken him. Perhaps it was because I knew, deep down inside, tucked away in the place where the real secrets lay hidden, that a tiny bit of the darkness was inside me now too.

"It's the only way to keep God in the hearts and minds of the people," he said. He'd moved his hand and I thought he was going to touch my feet again. I had to fight to ignore my craving for him to grab my toes and send away the cold. "You see, son, the true light of God lives in the world only because there is true darkness. A person can't know the light without knowing the dark, indeed, there can *be* no light unless darkness exists alongside it." His voice had taken on a hint of his Sunday preacher tone as he explained. "For God said, 'Let light shine out of darkness.' And he has shone in our hearts to give the light of the knowledge of the glory of God in the face of Jesus Christ." He tapped my leg as if that settled that.

He said he hadn't known the darkness wanted the Larsen girl from the rodeo or the Higgins boy at the Strawberry Festival. But he had been ready for the darkness to take Cici Martin. He would make things right from now on.

Before he left my bedroom that morning, my

daddy had made me swear on an actual Bible that the secret of the darkness would be protected. "It's the only way, son. It's a terrible thing and a beautiful thing all rolled into one. And seeing as we are God's creatures, it's *His* way, too. A man's only as good as his word, son. And like my own daddy said to me, I know you have a heart for God."

We prayed together for strength and I knew without him having to tell me that this was something to be filed under the heading of *Things We Won't Ever Talk About With Mama*.

A small part of me—the part of me spinning off in the other world on that other reality—knew I should tell. I pictured Sheriff Hayman's face in my mind and imagined sharing what I knew. But it didn't feel right. And I tried to imagine sharing this with Mama, but something inside told me that if I shared this with her, it would dim her light forever.

The other part of me knew it wouldn't be possible to tell a single living soul. Who would believe me if I told a story about the darkness from my grandpa's grave hole and my daddy and my icy feet? I bet that if I went spouting on about the darkness taking Cici it wouldn't be long before the men in their white coats would arrive and take me away to the padded confinement room like they did to old Mr. Halliday when they found him on Main Street wearing only his boxer shorts and a tinfoil hat going on about the aliens coming to abduct him again after the last time when they found him delirious and ranting on the sidewalk outside Jane's Hardware.

No, I wasn't going to tell about the darkness. He was my daddy, and a preacher, and a man of God. The darkness had chosen him to do God's work. And yet I struggled with the back and forth going on inside my mind. Why did the darkness have to take Cici? Why her? Why here in Fern Leaf? I went to church every Sunday, and sometimes on other days too. I saw all the people praying and singing, rejoicing that they had God in their hearts. Did we really need Cici to be missing in order to light that fire in the congregation?

Maybe the darkness didn't need to keep Cici forever. It was true that ever since she'd been taken it was like the amount of praying to God Almighty had doubled or even quintupled from what it used to be. That had to count for something. Anyone attending Sunday service last weekend would have no doubt that the light of God was alive and well in the hearts of the people of Fern Leaf. Maybe God could be satisfied with that.

I wanted to be a man of God too. What better path to righteousness than to help lift up the hearts of his people by answering their prayers? And so as I sat across the breakfast table from my daddy and lifted my glass for him to pour me more orange juice, I vowed silently to myself and to the good Lord above that the darkness would have to change its plans—just this once.

I was going to find Cici Martin and bring her home, answering prayers and making the light of God burn even more brightly in the hearts of the good people of Fern Leaf.

AFTER BREAKFAST, I went back to my bedroom and pulled out one of my small notebooks, like the one Sheriff Hayman carried in his front pocket to make notes when he interviewed people about crimes and such. A good investigator was organized, and if I was going to find Cici, I had to do this right.

I closed my eyes and made a mental map of all the places where Cici could be. I walked the streets in my mind, turning left and right, picturing all the shops and houses, the school, and the church that I knew so well.

She had to be close, because on the day she went missing, my daddy had been at the school festival with everyone else. So, wherever she was, it had to be nearby, but also somewhere out of sight. I wrote down all the possibilities in a tidy list in my notebook.

I rummaged through the drawer of my desk and pulled out the folded map of our county. I drew a line between the points I'd chosen to search. As it turned out, my list of possible hiding places was not as long as I thought it would be. The way I saw it, Cici had to be somewhere in a triangle formed by the school, the church, and the woods behind our house. As I connected those dots on the map, a chill ran over my body.

Our house fell inside the triangle. She could be right here for all I knew.

The realness of the situation crashed over me like an ocean wave. What would I do if I found her? I worked through my list but was unable to come up with any answers. It seemed to me that once I found Cici, I could just explain things to her about how my daddy was only doing God's work and she was an instrument of God's light. Then I would make her swear on a stack of Bibles not to tell. I pictured me sending her on her way, yellow hair bouncing along behind her as she hurried back to her family who would thank God for answering their prayers and for-sure-certain everyone in Fern Leaf would be back in church praying twice as hard at the next service.

A smile spread through me and lit me up from within. My daddy may be doing God's work, but if I had learned anything growing up as a pastor's son and a child of God, it was that He worked through us in mysterious ways. I was being called to this. I knew it like I knew the Lord's Prayer. You could file that under the heading of *Things That Remain God's Own Mysteries*.

I started my search in our shed. It stood back a ways from the house and angled a bit toward the street. The wide wooden doors swung open on squeaky hinges as I slipped inside. The shed was large, about the size to fit three cars, but we didn't use it to store the family vehicle. Inside, it was an orderly but cramped space and smelled of dust, and oil, and rotting grass. On one side, the wall was taken up by my daddy's workbench. The rest of the space was cobwebs and storage, and all the things that we used only once or twice a year.

I moved the lawnmower out of the way and stepped over a pile of cut boards my daddy had been saving to repair the back fence. The space under the wooden shelves was packed with boxes and crates overloaded with Christmas decorations, painting tarps, and gardening tools. I knocked on the walls and even tapped my feet along the dirt floor looking for a secret hollow, but in the end, there was no place here for Cici to hide.

During my search, I found a box of old photo albums from when my daddy was younger. I slid the box off the shelf and carried it to the workbench. I pulled out the album on top and leafed through stiff, black paper pages. The photos had been attached using thin metal corner tabs, and the images showed my father as a young boy. But it wasn't him I was interested in.

I recognized his father right away. He looked just like the picture Daddy kept of him on the mantle. I turned more pages until I found a close-up shot of my grandfather's face. I wondered if he had the darkness inside him when this shot was taken. My daddy looked old enough, I guess. I had no way to know.

When I turned the last page of the album, I put it aside and reached into the box for the next one. By the time I got through the last of the albums, I was sweating like a hog on a spit and from the noise emanating from my belly you'd have thought I was starving. I stacked the photo books into the box and shoved it back on its shelf.

The door creaked as I pushed it open to step outside into the still air.

"What are you doing, son?" My daddy stood facing me, inches away.

I jumped back and clutched my chest for fear my heart would hop right out. "I . . . Just looking . . ." I glanced to my left at the first thing and spotted a bucket of gardening tools. "For Mama's garden shears. For the roses." Just the other day Mama said she needed to prune back her roses from the front yard. They were growing over the trellis and the thorny branches were getting too close to the porch stairs. "I thought you were at the church preparing for vacation Bible school?"

He looked at his watch. "It's lunchtime. I came home to join you and your mama. She said you'd been out here for hours." There was no sign of the darkness in him as he watched me.

Had it really been hours? I wiped the dirt and sweat from my forehead as I tried to trace back through time. "Guess I got caught up in poking around."

He mussed my hair. "All right. Well, the shears

are up near the porch. I put them there this morning for your mama. I'm sure she'd appreciate you helping her with that chore."

"Yes, Daddy," I said.

"After lunch," he chided. He put an arm over my shoulder and we walked back to the house.

I'd never told a lie to my father before. It felt awful and like he saw right through me. If he did, he didn't let on. I said a silent prayer asking God to overlook my fibbing as me doing my part of His good work here on earth.

That night, we had a full moon. I waited until Mama and Daddy went to bed and even waited another hour to make sure they had fallen asleep before I opened my window sash and slid out into the night.

I checked my map and my list of possible hiding locations in the moonlight. There were three locations I could only check at night and be sure no one was likely to be around. I double-checked that my flashlight worked and tucked it into my backpack along with a pair of my daddy's leather work gloves.

The night was warm and the still air was full of the sounds of crickets and frogs that filled the dark —good things, summer things, living things. I pulled my trusty Picayune Kings AAA Baseball League cap down over my forehead and hurried across the yard.

The schoolyard was eerie at night. The tall metal slide cast a thick dark swath through the sky, and the swing chains squeaked as I brushed past. Everything that looked so harmless and friendly during the day seemed ominous and full of shadow.

I took out my flashlight and pointed the beam inside the windows as I walked around the outside of the school. The building had been mostly empty the day that Cici Martin went missing. Being that it was the end of the year carnival and everyone was outdoors, it was still a possibility that she had gone inside to get something or use the girls' room so nobody would have seen when the darkness came for her. I did two whole circles around the building, looking in every single one of those rooms, but there was no sign of anybody inside. The school was locked up tight as a bug in a rug.

I felt sheepish and silly that I had put the school on my list in the first place. But I had to be thorough. Sheriff Hayman always said that you can never assume anything when investigating; you have to clear your mind of any presumption. But it was clear that Cici wasn't inside the school.

Across the street from the school building stood

the water tower, the words Fern Leaf spelled out in big black letters. The water tower was on my list. There was a little work shed out near the tower, and the pump room was big enough for a person to hide inside as well. There was also a tiny crawlspace at the base of the tower that they used as a maintenance closet. I read all about it in the town paper last winter when they interviewed the public works chief and he explained how the water tower served all the residents of Fern Leaf.

I eyed the tower and pictured the outbuildings in my mind. I would have to get to that later, after I was finished at the school.

I pulled out my list and checked off the school and noted the next place to check. I made a beeline across the grass to the old trailer parked behind the school building.

Years ago, there was a fire in the science lab inside the school. In order to keep classes running, they brought in a trailer and taught science classes from there. Once they fixed the fire damage, classes moved back inside the building, but they kept the trailer. Sometimes they used it for art classes or just for storage. There was a lock on the door, but all us kids knew that the side window was broken and wouldn't latch.

I pulled over a trashcan, and pushed it up against the trailer under the window. I climbed up and slid inside.

Inside the trailer, everything was in deep shadow. I pulled out my flashlight and clicked it on. The light filled the space, making the shadows starker as they danced around the edges of my flashlight's beam.

The trailer itself was a big open space. There were cabinets along one wall and a chalkboard set up at the back. The desks and chairs had been moved out, and aside from a layer of dust, it was clean and orderly.

An owl hooted in a tree outside and I nearly jumped out of my skin. I steeled my nerves and closed my eyes, re-dedicating myself to my mission —to God's mission. I couldn't let fear overtake me. An old owl wasn't going to get in the way of God's work.

Nonetheless, I hurried as I checked every cabinet in the trailer. When I was done, I shimmied out the window and crawled along the outside, pulling at the lattice along the bottom of the trailer until I found the loose piece that could be pulled wide enough to get inside.

The space underneath the trailer was full of spiders and creepy crawlies. I didn't mind them so much as long as they didn't mind me. I moved along the underside of the trailer, looking for signs that someone had been here recently. If Cici Martin were hiding here, I would definitely find her.

I had just finished crawling around the perimeter when outside, grass crunched under heavy boots. My throat squeezed shut and my blood raced through my veins, making my palms so clammy I almost dropped my flashlight.

"Son? What are you doing out here?" My father's voice was calm and soft as ever, not an inkling of anger or surprise.

I couldn't speak. Was Cici nearby? Did I set off some kind of tripwire that raised an alarm that woke him and made him come find me?

"Son. Come on out of there." He stepped over to the loose piece of lattice and pulled it open for me.

I got to my feet and brushed the spider webs and dirt from my clothes, my eyes cast downward in shame and in fear.

He lifted my chin and waited until I looked him in the eyes. "I know what you're doing, and I think it's noble. It is a good thing to try to right what looks like a wrong. But there are just some things you don't understand fully, and I'm here to make sure you stay safe. Do you understand me?"

I blinked back tears. "Yes, sir."

"Oh, there is no need for tears, son. I understand what you're doing, and it means you have a good heart." He tapped my chest. "But that doesn't mean I approve."

We walked back in silence, his hand on my shoulder, my guilty eyes watching my feet. When we got back to the house, he tucked me into my bed, and stepped over to my window, and slowly slid it closed.

He turned to me. With his back to the window, his body appeared in silhouette against the light of the full moon. "There are things you don't yet understand about the duty we have to the darkness and God's light, son. I need to you trust me in this." The darkness swarmed around his head and in that moment, his eyes seemed to blaze in the shadow.

My feet turned to ice. I watched him as he left my room.

THE FOLLOWING MORNING, while Mama served breakfast, my daddy told me that he needed me to help him work at the church for the next two weeks.

"Seems we have more little ones than we can

handle at VBS. You can help with arts and crafts." His voice was soft and gentle as always; there was no hint that I was being punished, though I'm sure he was doing this so he could keep a closer eye on me. You could file that under the heading of *Things That Don't Need To Be Said*.

I decided to make the most of the situation. I left my investigation notebook and my map in my room, under my pillow, but I remembered there were a couple places at the church I could probably check.

As it turned out, my daddy never let me out of his sight. For the two weeks I worked at the vacation Bible school, every moment of it was spent on edge. By day, my thoughts seemed consumed with whether or not my daddy was spying on me. But every night at home, after lights-out, my thoughts always went back to Cici Martin.

I wondered if she was afraid. Was she hungry? Was she hurt? What was my daddy doing with her? As far as I could tell, he wasn't spending a lot of time with Cici, wherever she was. Between his church work as the pastor, and vacation Bible school where I was with him for hours every day, and the time he spent with us as a family, there didn't seem to be much time left over to sneak away.

I tried my best to obey him. I did. I understood

what he told me about the darkness, and how it was his duty to do what he was doing. But I just couldn't settle the thought in my mind. The whole town was out of sorts over Cici Martin's disappearance, and everyone continued to pray for her as well as the other two children missing from the nearby towns.

Everybody still talked about her when they dropped off the children at the vacation Bible school. And even little ones asked about Cici during arts and crafts. I followed the cue of the other adults and gathered the children to focus on Jesus and gluing the colorful plastic jewels onto the picture frames they were making for their parents.

It was two long weeks before vacation Bible school ended. As we walked home after that final day, my daddy told me I had done well. He said he appreciated my help and my maturity. I hadn't seen a hint of the darkness in him since that night in my bedroom, but that didn't mean I forgot about his warning or about Cici Martin.

That night, Mr. and Mrs. Martin came by to meet with my father for some counsel and to pray. Mama brought out some lemonade, and I was shooed off the porch. I hurried inside and crouched down by the front window so I could hear them talking.

Mister and Mrs. Martin talked about Cici, and

their broken hearts, and how angry they were at God for not bringing their daughter back. I stared in wonder as Mama clutched Daddy's hand in hers and they cried for the Martins. And these weren't no crocodile tears; my parents wept from their souls for the loss the Martins were enduring.

I listened as Daddy consoled the Martins and led them in prayer. He asked God for guidance and for Him to shine a caring light over their son Anthony who was home right now with his auntie watching over him.

Mama handed Mrs. Martin a tissue and refilled everyone's lemonade glasses. I watched them through the window and tried to balance the notion that my daddy could be such a good and Godly man even though he had the darkness right there behind his eyes. And surely, Mama was a woman of truth and goodness.

After the Martins left, my parents stayed outside, holding hands and rocking on the porch swing.

Mama's voice was light and pretty. "It's just dreadful, what they're going through. I couldn't imagine if someone had taken our boy. I simply don't know how I would carry on."

Daddy patted her hand. "Well, now, there ain't

nobody coming to take our boy. You shouldn't think such thoughts."

"How can you say that? Of course I think such thoughts. Everybody's thinking such thoughts. Whatever could have happened to little Cici? Until she is found, I don't know that I'll ever stop praying for her, thinking about her, and what it would be like if it happened to our family."

Daddy inhaled deeply and sighed. "God wants those prayers, for certain. But something tells me we may never know what became of little Cici. We're going to have to find a way to lay that burden down, give it up to God, and let him lighten our hearts."

"I suppose you're right, dear. It's just so dreadful."

"That may be true, but as the pastor and the pastor's wife . . ." He tapped her thigh. "It behooves us to put on a brave face. Lead by example. Bring the congregation together in solemn prayer. Search yourself and I bet you'll find that you can file that under the heading of *Things We Know In Our Hearts*, my love."

"Yes, of course. Of course, you're right, dear."

LATER THAT NIGHT, I waited in my bedroom. My

birthday was only three days away, and as a man of ten, I was getting old enough to make some of my own decisions. I waited until after dark, and I listened long for the sound of Daddy's snoring in the bedroom across the hall. Once I was sure he was deep asleep, and Mama along with him, I eased opened the latch on my window and slipped outside.

The night was completely dark under the new moon. I stood outside my window. The cool grass tickled the backs of my legs while my eyes adjusted. Something about the night without the moon made me feel like I had superpowers. I spied the raccoon along the edge of the woods. He didn't see me as he scrounged for food. Something rustled in the tree alongside the back of the house—a possum, maybe, or some other night creature. I didn't even need to pull the flashlight out of my backpack. And I didn't need to look at my list.

Something in my mind seemed to home in on Cici Martin. Maybe it was all that time spent so close to my daddy these past weeks. Maybe some of his thoughts had seeped out and had carried across the air to me like something from my science fiction comics. I couldn't explain it then and I can't explain it now, but somehow, I knew exactly which direction to head. I swallowed my fear of what would happen when Daddy found out I'd left and walked into the night.

Our house sat up near the road on almost two acres of land. We had neighbors on either side, and like everyone along this stretch of road, our property was long and narrow, and the backyard ended at the edge of the woods.

I waited another moment to be sure I was alone. Then I headed off into the backyard, toward the barbed wire fence near the tree line at the bottom of the low rolling hill. When I got about halfway through the yard, I turned right, behind the stand of walnut trees that grew on the side of the low hill and their dropped-fruit turned the ground inky black. Mama always warned me not to play in the grass under the walnut trees as she couldn't get the stains out of my clothes no matter how many times she washed them.

Around the side of the hill, surrounded by the rising earth, a root cellar had been carved into the ground. The metal entrance was angled like a cellar door and secured with a heavy padlock. I'd forgotten about the lock. I'd have to go back to the house and grab my daddy's key from the ring hook in the kitchen.

I turned to head back and bumped right into my daddy's chest. My heart sped up as I rubbed the sting from my nose.

He dangled the keys in the air between us, the metal tinkling in the night. "Looking for these, son?"

Under the new moon, the sky was full on black. Starlight was dulled by a mild haze, and provided no light at all. But as I gazed up at my daddy's face, I saw a darkness so deep, it made the rest of the night around us look like daytime and I understood what he meant about the darkness that made us crave the light.

I blinked, unsure how to proceed. He didn't seem angry. He seemed calm, like he was doing me a favor. "I'm sorry, Daddy. I couldn't help myself. I know you told me to obey you and stay indoors and not look for Cici Martin, but . . ."

He waved off my words as though they meant nothing. "Ain't no thing, son. Ain't no thing. Now that the moon has gone dark, it's the perfect time—the *only* time for you to be walking in the night." He handed me the keys, and stepped back, giving me some space to unlock the cellar door.

My hands shook as I took the keys; I had to grip them to keep them from jangling. My knees wobbled as I bent toward the lock. It was too dark outside.

Suddenly, I couldn't see very well at all. I fumbled in my backpack for the flashlight.

"No need for all that." My daddy put his hand on my shoulder. He took the keys from me and urged me aside as he moved toward the door. He lifted the padlock and inserted the key on one try and then opened the latch and discarded the lock in the grass.

My daddy reached down and grabbed the handles. The metal doors moved in silence on greased hinges, and as soon as they were open, the night filled with the smell of Cici Martin. My nose twitched, and the hairs on my body stood on end. And I know it sounds strange, but my mouth watered.

"It's all right, son, just go with it. Let it take you." He watched me take it all in. He didn't seem at all surprised. In fact, he seemed to expect it.

Something inside me bloomed into life. It was foreign, animal, and wild as the night. It was like a creature had come awake inside my body. It growled a low growl of hunger and rage. I didn't like the rage. I swallowed. "I'm afraid, Daddy."

"Close your eyes, son." His voice was like velvet in the night. "Listen to your heart and hear the truth of it." He gripped my shoulder and squeezed a little. "I know exactly how it feels right now for you. You're thinking that you won't come back from this. But you will. You have already. You can file that under the heading of *Things God Has Promised*."

Already? I had already? I fought with my mind, thinking back in time. I tried to recreate the timeline —but nothing was there.

"It will be hard for you to remember all of this come tomorrow. Trust me, I know. I'm pretty sure you don't remember the night at the rodeo, or your adventures at the Strawberry Festival. I think it's God's way of making this easy on you. But as time goes on, you'll start to keep some fragments of these memories and once that happens; once you know this is temporary, it won't be so frightening to let go."

I inhaled deeply, letting his words steep like tea into my mind. I had done this already? At the rodeo? At the Strawberry Festival? Could it be?

Then something inside me switched on, and I recognized the rightness of it, or perhaps the inevitability of it. There was no other way. This was the true path, the only way to keep God's balance. I was an instrument of the darkness—God's darkness. It was my purpose to spread the darkness in order to keep the light of God's love alive in the world.

No sooner had those thoughts moved through

my mind when they were replaced by the oddest sensation I've ever known.

I shrugged off my backpack and let it drop to the ground. Then I pulled my tee shirt over my head and got down on my hands and knees. I can't explain how it happened exactly, only that it did. One second I was staring at the hints of my pale hands in the meager light of the night, and the next second my hands morphed into hairy paws covered in fur darker than the deepest black.

The smell of Cici grew stronger as the beast woke up within me. The ice in my toes gave way to heat and strength, and I looked up at my daddy and felt like I had been drenched in understanding.

He stepped back and let me enter the cellar, his words echoing in the narrow stairwell. "We are a team, you and I, son. God's team. And we shall work together to make sure we can continue doing His holy work. I should have been more careful with you, with the other two. I should have been more diligent so as to protect you from yourself. I didn't know, and I am sorry for that. The transition to my new role for the darkness wasn't immediate. But I am here for you now."

There were no lights on within the cellar, and the earthen walls smelled dank and kept the air cool inside. With each step I gave a little more of myself up to the beast.

Cici's rapid heartbeat rang through the air like a bell. I inched toward her, one step at a time. As I closed in on my prey, I lost hold of my boy mind and fully became the beast.

Like my daddy said, I didn't remember much else about my time in the darkness; I never could hold on to much past the time of the transition. I thank the good Lord above for that mercy. But my last conscious thought was of thanks to my daddy who watched over me, guided me, and closed the cellar door behind me to make sure nobody would hear Cici Martin's screams.

THE REST of the summer rolled on as it always does. Talk of Cici Martin moved from the front of everyone's minds, and eventually, she became just another name on the list of children missing in the Tri-County area. Turns out Mississippi has one of the highest rates of missing children in the whole of the South, stretching back generations. It was a mystery to everyone, but my daddy and I knew that we could file that under the heading of *Things The Darkness Has Wrought.*

Daddy and I spent more time together, traveling to different churches and visiting the congregations peppered around our beautiful state. Our days were spent with him teaching me the ways of life as a pastor and me studying God's word so I could become the man I was supposed to be. Except for one night every four weeks or so when the moon disappeared and my world fell to the darkness. On that night, the beast emerged.

Daddy never knew ahead of time which child God would deem worthy of giving to the darkness, but as each new moon threw the night into shadow, I found myself able to satisfy the beast from the offering Daddy made in our cellar.

I'VE TALKED a lot about the darkness, but it's vital to understand this aspect of the law of nature under God. Just like good and evil are opposite sides of the same coin and joy and woe live only as reflections of each other, light simply cannot exist without darkness. And darkness is meaningless without the light.

A person could go their whole life living in the light, never knowing that the darkness is right alongside it—so close they could touch it. For some people, the light takes up the whole of their life. But for me and mine, the good Lord has seen fit to line our lives with shadow.

Many years have passed since those early days when the darkness brought the beast into me. I closed my eyes and readied myself to stand before the grave of my own daddy. I took in a deep breath and when I opened my eyes I found myself looking at my newly shined shoes. I smiled, picturing old memories.

I looked forward to watching over my son, and moving into the next phase of my own journey—where I could stop feasting for the darkness and instead, hunt for sustenance and protect my son as he moved into the first phase of his dance with the darkness.

Now don't you fear, this isn't to say that this life of ours is all darkness and woe. It most certainly is not. It's just that someone must be the bearer of the darker things in service to God's light. We are God's creatures. We have been chosen.

I reached for the door latch and let myself out of the car, holding it open for my boy. At twelve years old, he seemed so much wiser than I was when I met the darkness at age nine. I mussed his hair and squeezed his shoulder. It wasn't for me to question what was about to come. The good Lord above worked in mysterious ways—oh, yes he did. And you can file that under the heading of *Things That Are Just True*.

A NOTE FROM CORINNE O'FLYNN

Believe it or not, the genesis of this story came from a real event. While the true story did not entail a seeping darkness creeping from the grave nor any missing persons, it did have to do with an evil spirit that possessed someone, and impacted their family in disturbing ways. Of course, my mind exploded with the possibilities of how to develop this as a fictional story, and thus THINGS THAT ARE JUST TRUE was born.

I hope you enjoyed reading. Continue on for a sneak peek at another creepy paranormal story of mine: GHOSTS OF WITCHES PAST . . .

GHOSTS OF WITCHES PAST

CHAPTER ONE

WHAT WAS LEFT OF NIALL TOBIN SHIVERED AS HE waited under an elm tree just beyond the border of Tower Hill. He blew into his fists, his breath weaving like arctic fog through his fingers. Damn if the woman wasn't taking forever.

Icy rain fell heavily through the trees, thick drops causing low branches to dip down and brush his shoulders. He flinched with each touch as if the forest concealed countless chilly hands reaching from the darkness to snatch him and carry him home. And here he thought autumn in Ireland seemed miserable. He'd never felt the bite of October in New York's Hudson Valley before.

Looking down at his bare feet, pale and freezing, he

thought he'd never be warm again. Had he been able to plan properly, he would've worn a coat and shoes. But there'd been no time. He'd barely escaped as it was. Thank the gods, or whoever was looking out for him that Blackie, the old bartender, had taken pity on him.

Hiding in the shadows, he recalled his surprise the night before as his brothers had grabbed him from bed. How easily they had overpowered him and carried him down the stone steps to the crypt. How worried he'd been that Mother would discover they'd entered that part of the house. His shock at seeing Mother waiting by the altar. The greedy look on her face as they'd strapped him down and his own mother had woven the spell that stole his magic away.

At seventeen, and still a minor according to magical law, his power was under his parents' control. But that's why they picked him—his magic wouldn't be his own for another year. He was theirs to use.

When he was younger, he had yearned for his family to be like other families they knew. Most families didn't treat their children like animals. Most families ...

He'd been lucky to escape. But standing now in

the freezing rain, he wondered if he'd made a mistake in coming here.

He'd used the charm Blackie had given him to entrance a mouse to do his errand, pushing away the shame that he lacked the strength to spell something grander—like a cat or a raven—to such a simple chore. The message itself would have to be enough to make Prestiger Amber McClintock come out to meet him—a stranger—in the pouring rain. It had to work. She had to come.

He imagined her untying his note from the mouse's tail. Would she be surprised by the photo or would it make her angry?

He didn't know the woman in the picture, though everyone knew who Prestiger McClintock was. The legendary McClintocks of Tower Hill were one of the old families, held in the highest regard. And she was a ranking member of the ruling Prestigium who governed the magical world.

But none of that mattered. Amber McClintock was in the photo, so she'd been there that night. And she was the key Niall needed—an alternative witness for his family. Someone who could answer their questions. He'd have to convince her, but if she agreed to help him, he'd bring her back to his family and explain. With her help, they wouldn't have to kill him. With her, they'd have a witness that didn't require his death.

Another branch tapped its finger on his back. Niall's already racing heart jumped. He stole a quick glance over his shoulder. Damn the rain.

A light winked through the woods on the other side of the stone bridge. A hooded figure in a dark cloak stepped from the trees, wand held high. The glow from its tip transformed the rain into droplets of falling glass.

Niall held his breath. He didn't dare reveal himself until he knew it was her.

The figure stopped at the foot of the bridge and glanced around the small clearing. Niall felt well hidden, and no witch could sense his presence through the protective veil shielding the McClintock territory from outsiders. Still, he moved back deeper into the shadowed, clawing branches.

The figure stepped onto the bridge and moved to the center of the arch. Pale hands reached from under the cloak and pulled back the hood.

She was older than when the photo had been taken, but there could be no mistaking the mane of dark, curly hair and the angle of her chin. Prestiger Amber McClintock stepped through the veil, sending a momentary ripple across the air like dust motes glinting in the sun, though it was after midnight and pouring rain.

"Is someone there?" She raised her wand light as she scanned the forest. "I got your message, but I don't understand." She reached into her pocket and pulled out the piece of newspaper Niall had sent to her. Raindrops quickly dotted the page.

Niall stepped from the shadows. "I'm here."

She pointed her wand at him and retreated a step, the veil shimmering as she pierced its surface with her back. "Who are you? And what's wrong with you? I barely sense you there."

Niall raised his hands to show he wasn't armed and walked toward the woman on the bridge. His feet were so numb he could barely feel the cobbles beneath them as he stepped up onto the stone. "My name's Niall, ma'am . . . Your Honor. I need your help."

"This picture, where did you get it?" She looked worried, which he supposed was better than angry.

"My family—"

"Yes, what's your family name?" she demanded.

Here was the part he hated. The part where he could either be sent away or ignored. He clenched his teeth. "Tobin. I—"

"Tobin?" Prestiger McClintock's face flashed

anger. "What are you doing here? What do you want?" She retreated another step, safely behind the barrier, guarded now.

Damn his name. Damn it all.

He stepped forward. "I swear, I mean no harm. I've left my family. I'm not like them."

"Easy words to say, young man."

He tried again. "The picture. It's you."

"Yes, but I don't . . . It was taken a long time ago." She glanced over her shoulder into the darkness of the woods behind her. "You shouldn't be here."

"It was taken at the World Samhain Festival eighteen years ago," he said.

"What do you want from me?"

"You saw that man die."

She blinked, and her eyes glistened in the wand light. She looked like she might cry. "I don't—I can't remember anything from that time."

How could she lie about this? "You don't remember watching someone get murdered?"

She shook her head. "It was too painful. Those memories, they're gone . . . I don't . . ." She stopped talking, forehead creased in concentration.

This wasn't going well. How was she ever going to help him if she claimed to have no memory? She must be lying. She just didn't want to talk about it.

Niall stepped closer. "You were there. You witnessed. My grandmother was accused of murder. My family—we're outcast. My grandmother died without ever clearing her name. And now they're trying to kill me with some old spell . . ."

Prestiger McClintock stared at the old piece of newspaper, soggy now, and limp in her hand. "What do you know about this man? The one who died?"

"I know my family has found evidence proving my grandmother's innocence." He moved forward again, felt the tip of his nose touch the invisible barrier before him. "Alice Tobin was no murderer," Niall spoke the words his mother said so often they were like her mantra. He couldn't help but feel a twinge of pride, despite what his family had done to him.

She stepped forward, piercing the veil and clutching Niall's hand. "His name. Do you know his name?"

Niall flinched. Her touch was like a flame against his icy skin. Was she daft? Everyone knew the name of the man who was murdered at the London Samhain Festival.

"Ethaniel Morrison, and my family intends to—"

At the mention of the dead man's name, full tears

welled in Prestiger McClintock's eyes. Then a slow smile of recognition spread across her face.

"Ethaniel," she whispered.

Hope surged through him. "Yes! You do remember! I knew it!"

Something between them changed. Prestiger McClintock tensed and let go of Niall's hand. Her face went tight. She glanced over his shoulder. "You said you were alone."

"Oh, no." Without his full power, Niall had no way to sense the presence of another witch approaching. He followed the Prestiger's gaze and turned to look behind him. He saw nothing but the trees and the rain and the thick autumn woods.

"Who is with you?" She stepped backward, through the veil again.

"I'm alone. I swear it." Niall stepped to the barrier, hands pressed flat, as if against a wall of glass. "Wait, please! Let me in. Is someone coming?" His throat tightened in panic. He couldn't sense anyone. He could barely feel the witch standing directly in front of him, and she was one of the most powerful in the world. He didn't dare turn around again.

He could have been followed. Bloody hell.

He closed his eyes and felt for anything, even a

hint of another witch in the forest. This must be what it's like for regular humans, living their lives in the mundane world with no sense of the energy around them.

Petrified by his vulnerability, his mind painted an image in frightening detail. He pictured his brother, Colin—they would have sent Colin after him, for sure—with his black hair and his murky eyes. He'd be wearing that dark grin on his face, like a cartoon cat who'd finally caught the canary.

He imagined Colin stepping out from the cover of the trees, oblivious to the rain and the clutching branches. He'd draw his wand, ready to snag Niall in one of his oh-so-special snares, designed to strangle an animal to the point of submission. He'd drag Niall home so they could finish with him. Murder him.

Niall pictured it all.

Terror at returning to that crypt filled Niall's mind as he pressed his forehead onto the barrier. "Please." He clasped his hands in front of him. "Mrs. McClintock, they're going to kill me."

Prestiger McClintock raised the newspaper clipping, showing it to him a second time. "This man in the picture. Do you know his name?" she asked, eyes desperate. "What's his name?"

Niall felt his belly lurch at the repeated question. He searched her face but found nothing but genuine curiosity. It was as if she truly didn't remember hearing the man's name only moments ago.

A branch snapped behind him. He froze, unable to turn and look. He'd come so far . . .

"I'll tell you everything. All I know about Ethaniel Morrison. Please. Just let me in."

Relief washed over her face again. "Ethaniel," she whispered.

What the hell was going on? The woman was mental. Niall watched as her face flew through thoughts, brow flashing a worried crease and then a hardened scowl.

The whole time her eyes scanned the area behind him, seeking the person they both could hear approaching through the forest. Her jaw clenched as she appeared to settle on her decision.

Leaves crunched under footsteps behind Niall, first slowly, then more swiftly. From the sound, Niall guessed the person was very close, almost to the edge of the clearing. He couldn't turn to look. Instead, he held her gaze and braced for impact.

Amber McClintock's stare locked onto Niall's. "If this is a trick, you'll live only long enough to regret it." She reached into her collar and pulled a long chain over her head. She held out a rectangular, gold locket and said the words he needed so desperately to hear. "Take this as token, be welcome."

Niall snatched the locket. There was no turning back—his family would view this as the betrayal it truly was. He dismissed the thought. It didn't matter anymore. Besides, they betrayed him first, and this was life and death. *His* life and death. And he'd make everything all right.

Relief overwhelmed him that something, finally, had turned in his favor. He'd found an ally. Blinking back stinging tears, Niall bowed his head in silent thanks. He took a step toward the invisible barrier, skin too numb with cold to feel the shimmer as his face passed through it.

The footsteps stopped.

"No!" Prestiger McClintock gripped Niall by the shoulders and pulled him the rest of the way through the veil. He was so weak; she managed to throw him. He landed hard, the cobbles of the bridge tearing at his frozen hands.

He got to his feet and turned to see Prestiger Amber McClintock writhing in the air, fighting a stream of golden light that pulsed and burned brighter by the moment. Then she dropped to the ground like a rag doll. Around her, the light exploded.

The blast sent Niall sailing into the woods. His thoughts focused on his luck—that no matter what happened now, he was inside the veil's protection and beyond their attacker's reach. He watched in slow motion as the trees closed in around him, paying no mind to the branches as they grabbed him and pulled at his clothes. He was safe now. He was safe.

Then his head came into contact with the trunk of a tree, and all went dark.

ALSO BY CORINNE O'FLYNN

The Expatriates Series

Song of the Sending

Promise of the Scholar

Soul of the Sword (Coming 2018)

Witches of Tower Hill Series

Ghosts of Witches Past

The Aumahnee Prophecy Series

Eamonn's Tale

Marigold's Tale

Watchers of the Veil

Defenders of the Realm (Coming 2018)

Tales From the Veil Series

The Portal Keepers

The Gimcrackers

Short Stories

Suicide High *(TICK TOCK Anthology)*

One Final Death *(OFF BEAT Anthology)*

Things That Are Just True *(DEAD NIGHT Anthology)*

The Fog Queen *(Shiver Me Timbers Anthology)*

ABOUT CORINNE O'FLYNN

Corinne O'Flynn is a USA Today bestselling author of fantasy and mystery books. She's a native New Yorker who wouldn't trade life in the Colorado Rockies for anything. She loves scones and tea, and when not writing, she can be found hanging with her husband, their four kids, three dogs, playing board games, knitting, reading, or binge watching some fabulous shows (while sipping tea). Follow her online at http://www.corinneoflynn.com